U0099341

Story·a·Nigh

伍史利的大日記

—— 哈洛森林的妙生活 ——

Linda Hayward 著

本局編輯部 譯

三民書局

國家圖書館出版品預行編目資料

伍史利的大日記（Story a Night）
——哈洛森林的妙生活 II／Linda
Hayward 著.--再版.--臺北市：
三民，民88
　　面；　公分
ISBN 957-14-0191-9（精裝）

855

網際網路位址　http://www.sanmin.com.tw

© 伍史利的大日記
(Story a Night)
——哈洛森林的妙生活 II

著作人　Linda Hayward
譯　者　本局編輯部
發行人　劉振強
著作財
產權人　三民書局股份有限公司
　　　　臺北市復興北路三八六號
發行所　三民書局股份有限公司
　　　　地　址／臺北市復興北路三八六號
　　　　電　話／二五○○六六○○
　　　　郵　撥／○○○九九九八——五號
印刷所　三民書局股份有限公司
門市部　復北店／臺北市復興北路三八六號
　　　　重南店／臺北市重慶南路一段六十一號
初　版　中華民國八十五年二月
再　版　中華民國八十八年二月
編　號　S 85338

基本定價　捌元肆角

行政院新聞局登記證局版臺業字第○二○○號

有著作權・不准侵害

ISBN 957-14-0191-9（精裝）

July 1

Although summer days were hot, work still went on in Woods Hollow. The mothers and fathers were always busy.

It was Mother Squirrel's job to deliver the mail. Every morning she went from burrow to burrow, from cave to cave, from hollow tree to hollow log, putting letters into mailboxes.

The letters came from faraway places. Little chipmunks wrote to their cousins, Zip

夏天的日子雖然悶熱，但在「哈洛小森林」裡，一切工作仍然繼續著，爸爸媽媽們總還是很忙碌的喲。

松鼠媽媽的工作就是傳遞信件。每天早上，她得走過一個接一個的洞穴、地洞，或是空心圓木；就這樣不停的走著，把一封封的信件投進信箱裡。

這些信來自遙遠的地方：

and Kibby. Aunt and Uncle Raccoon wrote to their nephew, Rocky. Young ground hogs who lived in other parts of the forest wrote to Grandpa Ground Hog.

In the afternoon Mother Squirrel collected the mail.

Father Robin wrote to other birds. Mother Raccoon wrote to other teachers. Grandpa Ground Hog answered all of his mail, too. Mother Squirrel had to send these letters on their way.

Mother Squirrel had been working so hard that she was really looking forward to a holiday.

有小花栗鼠寫給他們的表兄妹茲普和姬碧的信，有浣熊伯母、伯父寫給姪子洛奇的信，也有住在森林另一邊的年輕土撥鼠寫給土撥鼠老爹的信。

到了下午，松鼠媽媽便得去收信。

有知更鳥爸爸寫給其他小鳥的信，有浣熊媽媽寫給其他老師的信，也有土撥鼠老爹寫給所有人的回信。

松鼠媽媽必須把這些信全送到該到的地方呢！

松鼠媽媽一直很努力的工作，她好盼望有個假期唷。

July 2

Father Raccoon was the forester in Woods Hollow. It was his job to look after the plants that grew there, especially the trees. Everyone who lived in Woods Hollow needed trees.

浣熊爸爸是「哈洛小森林」的森林管理員，他的工作是維護森林裡的植物，尤其是樹木。

每一個住在「哈洛小森林」的居民都很需要樹木喲。

樹木提供了住的地方。貓頭鷹貝弗迪的家就在「大青松」的頂端，松鼠芭菲就住在「橡樹」裡頭，河狸巴克則把樹砍下做成他的家——「比弗小木屋」。

樹木也提供了食物。水果、核果、種子、樹汁等所有這些東西都

The trees provided homes. Belvedere Owl's home was at the top of Tall Pine. Buffy Squirrel's home was inside Oak Tree. Buck Beaver had cut down trees to make his home, Beaver Lodge.

The trees provided food. Fruits, nuts, seeds, sap—all of these things came from trees.

The trees provided shade. The shade made it possible for young trees and shrubs and ferns and flowers to grow.

Father Raccoon checked the trees daily. He looked for pests like moths and beetles. They could harm trees. He looked for signs of fire. It could destroy trees.

Father Raccoon was also looking forward to a holiday.

來自樹木。

　　樹木還提供了陰涼的地方。陰涼的地方才能使小樹、灌木、羊齒植物和花朵等得以生長。

　　浣熊爸爸每天都來檢查樹木，他得找出蛾和甲蟲這一類的害蟲，因為牠們會傷害樹木呢。此外，他也要尋找任何可能引起火災的跡象，因為火會毀掉樹木呢。

　　浣熊爸爸也好盼望有個假期哨。

-------------------------------------- July 3

Mother and Father Chipmunk had their
work to do, too.

"Can you play with us today?" asked Zip
and Kibby.

Not on Mondays. On Mondays, Mother and
Father Chipmunk washed and mended the
clothes.

Not on Tuesdays. On Tuesdays, Mother and
Father Chipmunk baked and cooked the food.

花栗鼠爸爸和媽媽也同樣有工作要做喲。茲普和姬碧問:「你們今
天可以陪我們一起玩嗎?」

星期一不行!每個星期一,花栗鼠媽媽和爸爸要清洗和縫補衣服。

星期二不行!每個星期二,花栗鼠媽媽和爸爸要烘烤和烹調食物。

星期三不行!每個星期三,花栗鼠媽媽和爸爸要修理壞椅子和擦亮

Not on Wednesdays. On Wednesdays, Mother and Father Chipmunk polished the furniture and repaired broken chairs.

Not on Thursdays. On Thursdays, Mother and Father Chipmunk cleaned and swept and dusted the house.

Not on Fridays. On Fridays, Mother and Father Chipmunk made soap and candles and baskets and pots.

Mother and Father Chipmunk were certainly looking forward to a holiday.

家具。

　　星期四不行！每個星期四，花栗鼠媽媽和爸爸要清理房子、打掃屋子和拂去灰塵。

　　星期五不行！每個星期五，花栗鼠媽媽和爸爸要製造肥皂、蠟燭、籃子和鍋子。

　　花栗鼠媽媽和爸爸一定也好想有個假期呢！

On the Fourth of July the holiday that everyone had been waiting for finally arrived. Independence Day!

The Chipmunk family went to Snow Hill to celebrate. There were games and prizes and a noisy parade. There was dancing and singing and delicious food.

"Why is today a holiday?" asked Zip.

"Today is the day we celebrate our country's independence," explained Father Chipmunk.

"I like holidays because there are so many interesting things to do," said Zip.

"I like holidays," Kibby added, holding hands with Mother and Father Chipmunk as they danced in a circle, "because mothers and fathers don't have to work."

七月四日這一天，每個人等待已久的假期終於來臨了！今天是美國獨立紀念日。

花栗鼠一家人到「雪丘」上慶祝。他們玩遊戲、摸彩、熱鬧的列隊遊行，還有唱歌、跳舞和吃可口的食物呢。

「今天為什麼是假日呢？」茲普問著，

「今天是慶祝我們國家獨立的日子啊。」花栗鼠爸爸解釋。

　　茲普又說了，「我喜歡假日，因為可以做這麼多有趣的事情呢。」

　　「我也喜歡假日，」正和花栗鼠媽媽和爸爸手牽手，圍著圈圈跳舞
的姬碧也加了一句，「因為媽媽和爸爸都不用工作呀。」

　　蝌蚪泰弟正躺在「比弗池塘」沙沙的池底上，等待某些事情發生；
他等著變成一隻青蛙呢。

Tad Tadpole was lying on the sandy bottom of Beaver Pond. He was waiting for something to happen. He was waiting to turn into a frog.

But so far nothing had happened.

"I'll never be a frog." Tad sighed. "I'll never have big, bulging eyes. I'll never have a nice plump body. I'll never have long, powerful legs."

Just then he felt like wiggling to make himself more comfortable in the sand. But instead of feeling his tail wiggle, he felt something kick.

"Legs!" he cried. "I was so busy waiting to turn into a frog that I didn't even know I had grown two new legs. I'm going to be a frog after all."

但是，等到現在什麼都沒發生呀。

「我永遠都不會是隻青蛙了，」泰弟嘆了一口氣，「我永遠不會有又大又鼓的眼睛，不會有圓滾滾的好身材，也不會有強勁的長腿了。」

就在那個時候，他很想要扭一扭、動一動，好讓自己在沙堆裡更舒服些。但他感覺不到尾巴的擺動，反而覺得有某個東西在踢呀踢的。

「腿耶!」泰弟叫了出來，「我忙著等待變成一隻青蛙，卻不知道自己早就長出兩條腿了，我終於要變成一隻青蛙囉!」

July 6

Tad Tadpole was telling everyone he met about his new legs. That was all he could talk about. That was all he could think about.

"I have two legs," he told the big fish at the bottom of the pond.

"I have two legs," he told the little fish swimming near the shore.

蝌蚪泰弟逢人便說著他那兩條新長出的腿呢。他嘴裡講的就是這件事,腦袋裡想的也只有這件事。

「我有兩條腿了呢!」他告訴了池底的大魚;

「我有兩條腿了呢!」他告訴了在岸邊游泳的小魚;

「我有兩條腿了呢!」他也告訴了一條正扭扭擺擺經過的水蛇,碰巧這水蛇很會數數。

"I have two legs," he told the water snake as it wiggled by. But the water snake happened to be very good at counting.

"Wrong!" said the water snake. "You have four legs."

Tad was surprised to see that he had grown two more.

"I've been so busy telling everyone about my two *back* legs," he said, "I didn't notice that I had grown two *front* legs."

「不對喲!」水蛇說,「你有四條腿呀!」

泰弟驚訝的看見自己又多長了兩條腿。

「哎呀,我忙著告訴每個人我的後腿,」他說著,「卻沒注意到我也長了兩條前腿呢。」

Tad was having a wonderful time. He had never felt so good. He kicked his back legs. He wiggled his front legs. He stared all around Beaver Pond with his big, bulging eyes. A little fish swam by.

泰弟這陣子有著很美妙的時光，他從來都沒感到這麼滿意過。他踢踢後腿，划划前腿，用他一雙大而鼓的眼睛看著「比弗池塘」的每個角落。

一條小魚慢慢的游了過來。

"You're a funny-looking fish," said the fish. "Where are your fins? You don't even have a tail."

"I'm not a fish," said Tad proudly. "I'm a frog. Frogs don't have fins. Frogs don't have tails. Frogs are the handsomest creatures in the world."

"That's your opinion," said the fish, and she swam away.

「你這條魚長的真好玩,」這條魚說著,「你的鰭呢? 你甚至連尾巴都沒有啊?」

「我不是魚呢,」泰弟神氣的回答,「我是隻青蛙。青蛙沒有鰭,也沒有尾巴;青蛙是全世界最帥的動物唷!」

「那只是你的想法罷了。」這條魚說完就游走了。

　　茲普和姬碧想帶著他們的橡皮艇到「比弗池塘」去，但怎麼都找
不到呢！

　　「想想……」花栗鼠媽媽才張嘴，

　　「我們曉得了，」茲普和姬碧同時接著說，「想些別的事情做！」

　　「我們可以整理櫃子呀，」姬碧說，「當我們找不到東西時，我們

Zip and Kibby wanted to take their rubber raft to Beaver Pond but they could not find it.

"Think of—" Mother Chipmunk began.

"We know!" cried Zip and Kibby in unison. "Think of something else to do!"

"We could try cleaning our closet," said Kibby. "That's what we always do when we can't find something."

"And then we always find it in our closet," Zip said, laughing.

They ran to their closet and opened the door.

A rubber raft fell out and landed on top of them.

"I think we should name our closet the Lost and Found," said Kibby.

總是這麼做呀。」

　　「然後，我們總會發現東西就在櫃子裡呢。」茲普笑著說。

　　於是，兩個人趕緊跑到櫃子那兒打開櫃門，

　　一艘橡皮艇掉了下來，正好打到他們的頭。

　　姬碧說：「我想，我們的櫃子應該叫做『失物招領處』才對呢。」

July 9

Zip and Kibby carried their rubber raft to Beaver Pond. They set the raft down on the water. It floated nicely.

Kibby sat at one end. Zip sat at the other. They were just about to float away when Buffy came along.

"Can I go with you?" she asked.

茲普和姬碧帶著橡皮艇到了「比弗池塘」，他們把橡皮艇放在水中，橡皮艇便很平穩的浮了起來。

姬碧坐在一端，茲普坐在另一端，正要划走的時候，芭菲走過來了。

「我可以跟你們一起去嗎？」她問，

"Sure!" said Kibby. "There's always room for one more."

Buffy sat in the middle between Kibby and Zip. Zip pushed off with his oar. Kibby steered with hers.

And out toward the center of Beaver Pond went the rubber raft.

It was a very smooth sail.

「沒問題，」姬碧回答著，「總有多的位子呀。」

於是芭菲坐在姬碧和茲普的中間，茲普用槳把橡皮艇撐離岸邊，姬碧則用她那支槳來控制方向。

就這樣，橡皮艇快速的朝著「比弗池塘」的中央前進。

真是一次順利的航行呢！

Zip, Kibby, and Buffy were rowing their rubber raft around Beaver Pond when Buck swam up.

All of Buck's brothers and sisters swam up with him.

"What a nice raft!" said Buck.

"Climb aboard!" said Zip. "There's always room for one more."

"Hooray!" shouted all of Buck's brothers and sisters.

Buck and his brothers and sisters climbed onto the raft. Zip gave a push with his oar. Kibby steered with hers.

7 / 10

茲普、姬碧和芭菲划著橡皮艇在「比弗池塘」四處漫遊時,巴克游泳趕了上來。

巴克的弟弟妹妹們也跟著巴克游過來。

「好棒的橡皮艇唷!」巴克說著。

「上來呀!」茲普說,「總會有多的位子嘛。」

But the rubber raft did not go anywhere.
It just sank into the water.

「好耶!」巴克的十個弟弟妹妹都高興的大喊。

於是，巴克和他的弟弟妹妹們全擠上了橡皮艇。茲普使勁的用槳一划，姬碧用槳操縱方向，但橡皮艇並沒去任何地方呀!

它直接沈到了水裡。

姬碧和茲普正走過「比弗池塘」的時候，看見他們的朋友巴克把一條細細長長的木頭架在他的小船中央。

「你把旗竿架在船中央幹嘛?」茲普問了，

「這不是旗竿，」巴克回答，「這是船桅。船桅會把帆撐起來，我就要啟航了喲。」

Kibby and Zip were walking past Beaver Pond when they saw their friend Buck putting a long, slender piece of wood in the middle of his boat.

"Why are you putting a flagpole in the middle of your boat?" asked Zip.

"This is not a flagpole," said Buck. "This is a mast. The mast holds up the sails. I'm going sailing."

"Hooray!" cried Kibby. "Can we sail with you? Can I sit in the front of the boat?"

"The front of the boat is not called the front of the boat. It's called the bow. The back of the boat is called the stern. Everything in a sailboat has a special name."

"That's very interesting, Buck," said Zip.

"When I'm sailing, I'm called the skipper," said Buck.

「好耶!」姬碧高興的叫著,「我們可以跟你去航海嗎?我可以坐在前面嗎?」

巴克解釋了:「船的前面不叫『前面』,要叫『船首』;船的『後面』要叫『船尾』;帆船裡的每一樣東西都有特別的名稱呢。」「巴克,這聽起來挺有趣的呢。」茲普說著。

「當我在駕駛的時候,要叫我『船長』唷。」巴克說。

July 12

In the summer it was very warm in Woods Hollow. Everyone went to Beaver Pond to stay cool.

Rocky liked to jump into the water and make big splashes.

Buffy liked to wade.

夏天裡，「哈洛小森林」是非常悶熱的，每個人都到「比弗池塘」涼快涼快。

洛奇喜歡「噗」的一聲跳進水裡，濺起一大片的水花。

芭菲則喜歡在水中漫步。

茲普喜歡飄浮在水面上，假裝自己是一艘漂流的船。

Zip liked to float on top of the water and pretend to be a boat adrift on the ocean.

Kibby liked to swim.

"I can do the front stroke, the back stroke, the side stroke, and the frog stroke," said Kibby.

Tad poked his head out of the water and looked at Kibby.

"I can do the frog stroke, too!" he said. He gave a big kick with his back legs and a small push with his front legs—and swam away.

姬碧則喜歡游泳。

她說：「我會自由式、仰式、側泳及蛙式呢。」這時，泰弟的頭突然從水裡冒出來，他看著姬碧。

「我也會蛙式！」泰弟說完，就用兩條後腿使勁的一踢，兩條前腿往前輕輕的一划，就這樣游走了呢。

Buck was teaching his brothers and sisters how to be good swimmers.

"First you make fists with your front paws and hold them against your chest," said Buck.

Ten little beavers made ten little fists and held them against their chests.

7/13

巴克正在教他的弟弟妹妹們怎樣成為游泳好手。

「首先,把你們的前爪握成拳頭狀,抵在胸前,」巴克說著。

十隻小河狸各自握拳,抵在自己的胸前。

「然後,用你們的兩腿在水中來回踢著,」巴克接著說,「這樣就會使你們向前。」

"Then you push your feet back and forth in the water," said Buck. "That makes you go forward."

Ten little beavers pushed their feet back and forth in the water—and they all went forward.

"But how do we make ourselves go where we want?" they wanted to know.

"That's easy when you're a beaver," said Buck. "Just use your tail to steer."

　　十隻小河狸跟著在水裡來回踢著他們的雙腿，他們真的全都往前去了。

　　「可是，我們要怎麼讓自己游到想去的地方呢?」小河狸們都好想知道呢。

　　「這對河狸來說很簡單的，」巴克回答，「就用你們的尾巴來指揮呀。」

"Tell us a story," said Zip.

"Once upon a time," said Father Chipmunk, "there was a lovely white flower called Water Lily. All flowers like water, but Water Lily loved the water in a very special way.

「說個故事給我們聽聽嘛。」茲普說。

「從前，」花栗鼠爸爸開始說了，「有一朵可愛的白花，她叫做睡蓮。所有的花都很喜歡水，但是睡蓮喜愛水的方式非常特別唷。」

「有些花喜歡生長在樹林裡，只要在雨天裡能接觸到水就很開心了，但睡蓮可不喜歡這樣子。還有些花喜歡生長在河邊或池塘邊，只

"Some flowers were happy to grow in the woods and feel the water on a rainy day. Not Water Lily! Some flowers were happy to grow next to a river or a pond and look at the water from the shore. Not Water Lily! Water Lily wanted to be surrounded by water.

"And that is why," said Father Chipmunk, "the water lily floats on the top of the pond."

The water lily is the Flower of the Month for July.

要能從岸邊看見水就很開心了，但睡蓮也不喜歡這樣子呢。睡蓮想要讓水圍繞在她的四周哪！」

　　「這就是為什麼，」花栗鼠爸爸又說，「睡蓮都是浮在池塘上的原因唷。」

睡蓮是代表七月的花朵

「我喜歡夏天這種暖和晴朗的日子，」貓頭鷹貝弗迪說著，「每一天都讓人好舒服呢；沒有冰、沒有雪、沒有雨……」

這時候，貝弗迪恰好抬頭看了一下天空，他的頭頂上正有著好大的烏雲，這樣又黑又大的雲通常都表示著要下雨囉。

"I love the warm, sunny days of summer," said Belvedere Owl. "Every day is pleasant. There's no ice, no snow, no rain . . ."

At that moment Belvedere happened to look up at the sky. Overhead there were big, dark clouds. Big, dark clouds usually meant rain.

Just then he saw a bright streak of light flashing. A bright streak of light usually meant lightning.

Then he heard a low rumbling sound. A low rumbling sound usually meant thunder.

Dark clouds, lightning, thunder! What did Belvedere think about that?

"It can't rain," thought Belvedere. "This is summer."

　　說時遲那時快，他看見一道耀眼的亮光一閃而過，這一類的亮光通常就是指閃電了。

　　接下來，他聽見了一陣低沈的隆隆巨響，這樣的隆隆巨響就代表打雷了。

　　烏雲、閃電、雷聲！貝弗迪會怎麼想呢？

　　「不可能下雨呀，」貝弗迪想著，「現在是夏天耶。」

The weather expert of Woods Hollow was sitting in his weather station at the top of Tall Pine, watching the rain fall.

It was falling to the left of him. It was falling to the right of him. It was falling on top of him, too.

Belvedere decided to make a weather prediction.

"I predict rain," said Belvedere. "You are probably wondering why I predict rain, since it never rains in the summer. Well, there are big, dark clouds. There is lightning and thunder. These are signs that it is going to rain.

"And then, of course," said Belvedere, staring down at the puddles all around him, "there is one more sign I can scarcely ignore. I am getting wet."

7/16

「哈洛小森林」的氣象專家貝弗迪正坐在「大青松」頂上的氣象臺裡，看著雨滴落下來。

雨落在他的左邊，落在他的右邊，甚至也落在他的頭頂上。

貝弗迪決定做個氣象預報。

「我預測會是個雨天，」貝弗迪說了，「也許你們會好奇，為什麼

我會預測雨天呢？畢竟，夏天從來不下雨的呀；但是目前烏雲密布、
雷電交加，這些都是即將下雨的跡象。」

「當然，」貝弗迪眼睛盯著他底下四周的積水繼續說著，「還有一
個我無法忽視的跡象……那就是我全身上下都弄濕了。」

July 17

One day in July, Tad poked his head out of Beaver Pond and looked around.

"Hey, what smells so good?" he asked a frog who was sitting on a rock.

"Air!" answered the frog. "You can breathe it. You can jump around in it. You'll like the air."

Tad jumped up into the air and landed on a rock.

7 / 17

七月的某一天，泰弟把頭伸出「比弗池塘」的水面，向四處瞧瞧。

「嗨，是什麼東西聞起來那麼舒服啊?」他問著一隻坐在石頭上的青蛙。「空氣呀，」那隻青蛙回答，「你可以呼吸到空氣，也可以在空氣中翻翻滾滾，你會喜歡空氣的!」

泰弟用力往空中一跳，然後落在一塊石頭上。

"You're right," he said to the other frog. "I like the air. It feels good. But I like the water, too."

And Tad jumped—*kerlop*—back into Beaver Pond.

「你說的對,」他對另外一隻青蛙說,「我喜歡空氣,感覺很舒服,但我也喜歡水呀。」

泰弟噗通一聲,又跳回「比弗池塘」裡。

Tad wanted to go for a long hop in the woods. He wanted to have an adventure.

While he was wondering which way to go, he looked up and saw a big frog staring down at him. The big frog looked just like Tad—only bigger.

"Hi, I'm Tad," said Tad. "Who are you?"

7 / 18

泰弟好想來一次冒險，他想要在森林內做長途跳躍。

當他正在納悶該走哪一條路時，他抬起頭卻瞧見一隻大青蛙盯著他看呢。這隻大青蛙看起來和泰弟一模一樣，只不過大了一些。

「嗨，我是泰弟，」泰弟說，「你是誰呀?」

「叫我爹地就行了。」青蛙爸爸說。

"Just call me Dad," said Father Frog.

"Say, Dad," said Tad. "I need some advice. I am planning to go for a long hop in the woods. Which way should I go?"

"I have just one piece of advice for you, Tad," said Father Frog. "Stay here! A frog should stay near the water."

「是這樣的，爹地，」泰弟說，「我需要一點建議。我正打算在森林內來一次長途跳躍旅行，我該走哪條路呢?」

「泰弟，我只有一個建議給你，」青蛙爸爸說，「待在這裡! 青蛙就應該待在靠近水的地方啊。」

July 19

Tad wanted to follow his father's advice and stay near the water, but he also wanted to see what he could find in the woods.

"I will just go a short distance," he said.

He hopped and he hopped and he hopped—and soon he found himself in the woods. He began to feel very tired. He began to feel very dizzy. His skin was dry and tight.

泰弟很想聽從他爸爸的建議留在靠近水的地方，但他也想看看自己會在森林裡找到些什麼東西。

「我只要走一小段就好了。」他說。

於是他便跳呀跳，跳呀跳；沒多久，便發現自己在森林裡了，但泰弟開始覺得好疲倦唷！他感到頭昏眼花，就連皮膚也變得又乾又緊。

"I will hop into the water and get wet," he thought.

But there was no water in the woods.

So Tad slowly hopped back to Beaver Pond, where he was certainly glad to be in the water once more.

"Dad was right," said Tad. "Frogs should stay near the water."

「我得跳到水裡把自己弄濕才行。」他想著。

但森林裡並沒有水呀。

所以泰弟又慢慢的跳回「比弗池塘」去。在那兒，他真的很高興能再次泡到水裡呢。

「爹地說的很對，」泰弟說，「青蛙就應該待在靠近水的地方。」

July 20

Snow Hill was the highest point in Woods Hollow.

From the top of the hill one could see in every direction. There were no trees on Snow Hill to block the view.

In the winter Snow Hill was covered with snow. Then it became the perfect place to go sledding.

「雪丘」是「哈洛小森林」最高的地方。

從丘頂上能看見每個角落，丘上沒有樹木會阻礙視野唷。

冬天的「雪丘」蓋滿了白雪，這使它成為滑雪最佳的場地。

In the summer Snow Hill was covered
with grass. Then it became the perfect place
to go picnicking.

But it was still called Snow Hill—even in July!

Places are a lot like people. They keep the
same name all year around.

夏天的「雪丘」卻是綠草如茵，這時它又成爲踏青野餐的好地方！
然而，它卻一直被稱爲「雪丘」──即使是在炎熱的七月呢。
原來地點和「人」很類似，它們一年四季都是一樣的名字呢。

夏季的某一天，姬碧說：「讓我們到『雪丘』野餐吧！」

花栗鼠媽媽把野餐用的籃子找出來，他們在籃子裡塞滿了好吃的東西——水果啦，堅果啦和各種布丁。

花栗鼠爸爸把一個保溫瓶裝滿了冰涼又提神的水果酒。

然後他們爬上了「雪丘」頂。這裡陽光閃耀，微風輕吹；他們在

One summer day Kibby said, "Let's have a picnic on Snow Hill."

Mother Chipmunk found the picnic basket. They filled it with good things to eat—fruits and nuts and seed pudding. Father Chipmunk filled a Thermos with cool, refreshing punch.

Then they climbed to the top of Snow Hill. The sun was shining. A breeze was blowing. They spread their picnic blanket on the grass and sat down to eat.

"Eating *above* the ground is fun," said Kibby.

"We're not just eating above the ground," said Father Chipmunk. "We're eating above all of Woods Hollow."

草地上鋪開野餐用的餐巾，坐下來吃東西。姬碧說:「在高處吃東西挺好玩的。」

「我們不只是在高處吃東西喔，」花栗鼠爸爸說，「我們是在『哈洛小森林』的最高處吃東西呢!」

July 22

From the top of Snow Hill one could see in every direction. The Chipmunk family sat and looked out over all of Woods Hollow.

To the north was Beaver Pond. The blue water sparkled in the sunlight.

To the south was Stone Ledge. The many trees and bushes made it a dark, shady place.

從「雪丘」的頂端可以看向任何地方，花栗鼠一家人就坐著眺望整個「哈洛小森林」。

往北看，是「比弗池塘」；藍藍的池水在陽光下閃耀著。

往南看，則是「大岩崖」；許許多多的樹木和灌木叢使得那兒成為一個幽暗陰涼的地方。

To the east they could see Tall Pine, where Belvedere Owl was always standing alert for any change in the weather.

And to the west they could easily find their own neighborhood. There was Kibby's favorite apple tree and—not too far away—Oak Tree, where Buffy lived.

"North, south, east, west—looking toward your home is best," said Mother Chipmunk.

　　往東看，他們能看見「大青松」；貓頭鷹貝弗迪總是站在那兒監看天氣的變化呢。

　　最後往西看去，他們可以很容易就找到他們家鄰近的地方；有姬碧喜歡的蘋果樹，不遠的地方還有芭菲住的「橡樹」哩。

　　花栗鼠媽媽說了，「不論北、南、東和西，只要能看見自己的家就是最棒的了。」

July 23

Buck Beaver was fishing when Rocky came along.

"Sit here beside me," said Buck, "and I will show you how to fish."

He held up a fishing pole and a box full of equipment.

當河狸巴克正在釣魚時，洛奇走了過來。

「坐在我旁邊吧，」巴克說，「我來為你示範如何釣魚。」

他拿起一根魚竿和一個裝滿用具的盒子。

「首先，」巴克說，「你得要有一根竿子。然後，還需要一些鉛垂啦、浮標啦、釣絲上的蚊鉤啦、釣魚鉤啦等等的東西。你還得考慮線纏在一起時該怎麼辦，哪種餌最好；水流、氣溫都得要研究，你還要……」

"First," said Buck, "you need a pole. Then you need some sinkers, some bobbers, some leaders, and some hooks. You have to think about tangled lines and the best bait. You have to study the currents in the water and the temperature of the air. You have to—"

"Gee," interrupted Rocky. "I could never remember all of that. It's lucky I'm a raccoon."

"What do you mean?" asked Buck.

"Raccoons fish differently," explained Rocky. "I'll show you."

With that, Rocky stepped into the pond and scooped up a fish!

"We just grab them," said Rocky.

　　「哇嗚!」洛奇打斷他的話,「我哪能記得這麼多啊, 還好我是隻浣熊。」

　　「怎麼說?」巴克問,

　　「浣熊釣魚的方法很不一樣呢,」洛奇解釋,「來, 我示範給你看!」

　　話剛說完, 洛奇已踏進池塘裡用手舀起了一條魚。

　　「我們就用抓的。」洛奇說。

Zip and Kibby were walking by Beaver Pond one morning when they saw their friend Woodsley Bear. He was sitting on a rock, fishing.

"Hi, Woodsley," said Kibby. "Do you want to ask us any questions for your book?"

"I'm not asking questions today," said Woodsley.

"Then you must be *writing* the book today," said Zip.

"No, I am not writing today, either," said Woodsley.

"I know!" cried Kibby. "You are *thinking* about the book."

"No," said Woodsley. "I am thinking, but not about the book."

"What can you be thinking about besides the book?" asked Zip.

一天早上，茲普和姬碧在「比弗池塘」旁散步時，看見他們的朋友大熊伍史利正坐在石頭上釣著魚呢。

「嗨，伍史利，」姬碧說，「你想不想為你的書問我們問題呢?」

「我今天不問問題。」伍史利說。

「那你今天一定要寫書囉?」茲普說，

「不，我今天也不寫書。」伍史利回答。

Woodsley looked at his fishing pole and at his line dangling in the water.

"Fish," said Woodsley.

「我懂了，」姬碧叫著，「你是在想關於書的事情？」

「不，」伍史利說，「我是在想事情，但不是關於書的事情呢。」

「除了書以外，你還會想些什麼呢？」茲普問，

伍史利注視著他的魚竿和在水裡晃動的魚線，「魚啊！」他回答。

July 25

There were flies and more flies at Beaver Pond.

There were dragonflies, damselflies, fireflies, and butterflies. There were mayflies, crane flies, sawflies, and fruit flies. They zipped and darted and buzzed about.

"The flies are bothering us," complained Buck Beaver's ten little brothers and sisters.

「比弗池塘」有多到數不清的小飛蟲，像是蜻蜓、豆娘、螢火蟲、蝴蝶等；也有小一點的蜉蝣、長足蠅、鋸蠅和果蠅。

他們到處猛衝亂飛，而且嘶嘶亂響，嗡嗡亂叫。

「這些小飛蟲煩死了！」河狸巴克的十個弟弟妹妹這樣抱怨著。

「要趕走小飛蟲，對河狸來說是最簡單的事，」巴克說，「只要用

"It is the easiest thing to get rid of flies when you're a beaver," said Buck. "Just use your tail."

Buck thumped his tail on the water and all of the flies flew away.

Tad was sitting on a rock nearby, waiting for his dinner to buzz by.

"Why would anyone want to *get rid of* flies," he wondered, "when they are so good to eat?"

你們的尾巴就行了。」

巴克砰的一聲,把尾巴拍打在水面上,所有的小飛蟲便紛紛飛走。

泰弟坐在附近的一塊石頭上,等著他的晚餐嗡嗡的飛過來。

「怎麼會有人要把小飛蟲趕走呢?」他感到奇怪,「牠們好吃得很呢!」

Buffy was looking for her friends Zip and Kibby. They had said they would meet her at their apple tree.

Buffy walked three times around the trunk of the apple tree, but she did not see Zip and Kibby.

"We're up here!" cried Kibby.

Buffy looked up, but all she saw were lots and lots of green leaves.

"I can't see you," she said.

"We are sitting under the leaves," said Zip. "An apple tree is a very shady place to be."

"If this is an apple tree," said Buffy, "where are the apples?"

芭菲到處在找她的朋友茲普和姬碧,他們倆說好會在蘋果樹和她見面的呀。

芭菲在蘋果樹下繞了三圈,都沒有看到茲普和姬碧。

「喂,我們在上面這裡!」姬碧大叫。

芭菲抬頭看上去,看到的都只是密密麻麻的綠葉。

「我看不到你們啊。」她說了。

「我們坐在樹葉下,」茲普說,「蘋果樹裡好陰涼唷!」

7/26

"They're here, too,"
said Zip. "They are
very small and hard
and green. They are just
starting to grow."

Buffy looked very
carefully. She saw Zip,
she saw Kibby, *and* she
saw the little green
apples.

「如果這是蘋果樹，」芭菲說，「那蘋果在哪裡?」

「它們在這裡呀，」茲普說，「它們還非常小，又硬又綠，才剛開
始長呢。」

芭菲睜大了眼睛仔細的看，終於看到茲普、姬碧，也看到了那些
小小綠綠的蘋果了!

One day Zip and Rocky went on a hike.
Mother Chipmunk filled their knapsacks with
good things to eat.

"When we get to Stone Ledge," Zip said to
Rocky, "we will eat our lunches on a rock
near your home."

Zip and Rocky hiked along until they came
to Beaver Pond. There they decided to sit
down and have some snacks.

7 / 27

有一天茲普和洛奇要去健行，花栗鼠媽媽把他們的背包塞滿了好
吃的東西。

「等我們到達『大岩崖』的時候，」茲普對洛奇說，「我們就在你
家附近的岩石上用午餐。」

茲普和洛奇沿路走著，走到了「比弗池塘」。他們決定在那裡坐下
來休息休息，吃些點心。

Then they went on until they came to Tall Pine. There they decided to stop again. They opened their knapsacks and had some more snacks.

Then they went on until they came to Snow Hill. At the top of the hill they sat down, opened their knapsacks, and had still more snacks.

Finally they came to Stone Ledge. But when they sat down to eat their lunches, they discovered that their knapsacks were empty. They had already eaten their lunches!

Fortunately Mother Raccoon refilled their knapsacks with more good things to eat.

然後他們繼續走著，一直走到「大青松」。在那裡，他們又決定停下來休息；而且翻開他們的背包，再吃一些點心。

接著又繼續走，一直走到了「雪丘」。他們在「雪丘」頂上坐了下來，打開背包，又吃了一些點心。

最後，他們終於走到了「大岩崖」。但就在他們坐下來要吃午餐的時候，竟然發現他們的背包裡空空的。原來，他們早把午餐吃掉了！

幸好，浣熊媽媽又在他們的背包裡塞滿更多好吃的東西呢。

July 28

When nighttime came to Woods Hollow, it came slowly.

First the ground grew dark under the trees, and the creatures who lived there knew that nighttime had come.

The birds who lived up in the trees could still see the light in the sky. But later, when the sky grew dark, the birds also knew that nighttime had come.

黑夜總是緩緩的降臨「哈洛小森林」……

　　先是樹蔭掩映之下的大地逐漸暗了下來，住在那一帶的動物就知道夜晚來了。

　　住在枝椏上的鳥兒，雖然仍看到天空中的光亮，但當天色不久也轉暗時，鳥兒也就知道夜晚來了。

Because the moon shone down on Beaver Pond, Buck could see to work at night—and he often did.

Zip and Kibby were asleep in their burrow, but up above the ground, above the trees, one of their friends was wide awake.

Belvedere Owl, with his wings outstretched and his big eyes shining, was making his usual nighttime flight.

月光照在「比弗池塘」上，因此巴克可以在夜晚看見事物，還經常在夜裡工作哪。

地洞中的茲普和姬碧已睡得香甜，然而大地的上方，樹木上頭，他們的一位朋友卻是清醒著喲。

貓頭鷹貝弗迪張著翅膀，睜著雙眼，正展開他例行的夜間飛行呢！

「我們來升個營火吧,」大熊伍史利說,「但首先我們得收集些木柴。」於是大夥便分頭去找樹枝和樹皮。

「哎呀,我從沒有收集過木柴呢,這真是個好主意!」芭菲心裡想著。

"Let's make a campfire," said Woodsley Bear. "First we have to collect some firewood."

Everyone scattered to look for twigs and bark.

"Goodness!" thought Buffy. "I have never collected firewood before. What a great idea!"

She found a nice long branch and an interesting short one. She found twigs of different sizes. She found pieces of bark and strips of wood.

She carried everything back to the camp and put it into her knapsack.

"Why are you putting the firewood in your knapsack?" asked Kibby. "We need it to make a fire."

"I thought we were supposed to *collect* firewood," said Buffy.

"That's right," said Kibby. "First we collect it. But after that, we *burn* it."

她找到了一根很棒的長樹枝和一根很可愛的短樹枝，還找到不同大小的小樹枝和不少的樹皮和木片呢。

她把每一樣東西通通搬回營地，並且全裝進她的背包裡。

「妳幹嘛把木柴都放進背包裡呢?」姬碧問，「我們要它來生火耶。」

「我以為我們要收集木柴呢，」芭菲說。

「沒錯，」姬碧說，「我們是要收集木柴，但是接著我們要把它燒掉呀。」

Zip and Kibby and their friends were sitting around the campfire. As they watched the flames flicker, Woodsley Bear told a ghost story.

"Once there was an old deserted swamp," said Woodsley. "Nothing lived there. Nothing grew there. Nothing came there."

Everyone moved a little closer to Woodsley Bear.

"One night a heavy mist hung over the swamp," said Woodsley. "It was very still—too still."

Again everyone moved a little closer to Woodsley Bear.

"Then suddenly there was a low moaning sound," Woodsley continued, "as if a ghost were moving through the mist—closer, closer . . ."

姬碧、兹普和他們的朋友們圍坐在營火旁，正當大夥看著明暗不定的火焰時，大熊伍史利說了個鬼故事。

「從前有一個老舊荒蕪的沼澤，」伍史利說，「沒有人住在那兒，沒有生物長在那兒，也沒有人到過那兒。」

每個人都往伍史利身邊移近一點。

「有一天晚上，一陣濃霧籠罩住整個沼澤，」伍史利說，「沼澤變

　　But by this time no one could move any closer to Woodsley Bear. They were already sitting right in his lap!

得好安靜好安靜──簡直就是太安靜了。」

　　每個人又往伍史利身邊再移近一點。「突然間,傳來一陣低沈的呻吟聲,」伍史利繼續說著,「就好像有鬼在霧中移動,愈來愈近,愈來愈近……」

　　但這一次,沒有誰還能往伍史利身邊再靠近一點;

　　因為,他們都已經坐在伍史利的大腿上囉!

July 31

One night in July, Kibby and Zip did not sleep in their burrow underground. They slept on the ground, under the sky.

In the winter it was much too cold to sleep outside. But in the summer the air was still warm at night.

Kibby and Zip lay in their sleeping bags, but they could not fall asleep. There was so much to see, so much to hear.

七月的一個晚上，姬碧和茲普沒有睡在他們地底下的洞穴裡，而是睡在露天的地面上呢。

在冬天，天氣實在冷得沒法睡在戶外；但在夏天，晚上的氣溫仍然很溫暖。

姬碧和茲普躺在他們的睡袋裡，但就是睡不著，因為有太多的東西好看，太多的聲音好聽呢！

They could see the stars and the moon.
They could see the bats darting back and
forth between the trees. Then they saw a big,
familiar shape flying high above the trees.

It was Belvedere Owl!

They could hear the animals who were
awake at night moving through the bushes.
They could hear the frogs croaking at Beaver
Pond. One frog was making more noise than
all the rest.

That was Tad!

他們可以看到星星和月亮，

也可以看到蝙蝠在樹木之間快速的來回穿梭著。

然後，他們看見了一個巨大且熟悉的身影在樹梢上高飛而過，那
是貓頭鷹貝弗迪呢！

他們還可以聽到那些夜行動物在灌木叢裡走動的聲音，

也可以聽到青蛙在「比弗池塘」的呱呱叫聲。有一隻青蛙叫得比
其他的青蛙還大聲，那正是泰弟呢！

August 1

Zip and Kibby were sitting on the bank of Beaver Pond, enjoying the hot sun, when a little frog hopped out of the water and sat down beside them.

"Hi! I'm Tad," said the little frog. "Who are you?"

"I'm Zip," said Zip. "And this is my sister, Kibby. We live in the woods."

"In the woods?" Tad looked puzzled. "How do you stay wet?"

茲普和姬碧坐在「比弗池塘」的岸邊，享受著溫暖的陽光時，一隻小青蛙跳了上來坐在他們兩位的旁邊。

「嗨！我是泰弟，」這小青蛙說，「你們是誰呢？」

「我是茲普，」茲普說，「這是我妹妹姬碧，我們住在森林裡。」

「森林？」泰弟一臉困惑的問，「那你們要怎麼經常保持濕濕的呢？」

"We don't have to stay wet," said Kibby.
"We're chipmunks."

"Frogs have to stay wet," explained Tad.
"I'm a frog."

"How do you stay wet?" asked Zip.

"Watch!" cried Tad, and he hopped back
into the water.

「我們不必保持濕濕的呀,」姬碧說,「我們是花栗鼠。」
「青蛙就必須保持濕濕的呢,」泰弟解釋,「我就是隻青蛙。」
「那你怎樣保持濕濕的呢?」茲普問,
「看著喔!」泰弟大叫一聲,然後就跳回水裡去。

---------------------------------- August 2

Tad went to have a chat with Father Frog.

"Say, Dad," said Tad. "I need some advice. Which is the best place for me—land or water?"

"Where do you feel most comfortable?" asked Father Frog.

"Well," said Tad, "when I am in the water, all I can think about is how great it feels to be on land. On land I can hop and catch flies and bask in the sun. But when I am on land, all I can think about is how great it feels to be in the water. In the water I feel safe. Water feels like home."

泰弟找青蛙爸爸聊天去。

「是這樣的，爹地，」泰弟說，「給我些建議吧。到底哪個地方最適合我呢？陸地或是水裡？」

「哪裡讓你覺得最舒服呢？」青蛙爸爸問，

「這個嘛……」泰弟說，「我在水中的時候，想的都是在陸地那種

"I have just one piece of advice for you,
Tad," said Father Frog. "Stop trying to choose.
Frogs can live in both places."

很棒的感覺：我可以蹦蹦跳跳，抓抓小蒼蠅，做做日光浴；但在陸地
的時候，想的卻又是在水中那種美好的感覺：我在水裡會覺得很安全，
它就像個家一樣。」

　　「泰弟，我只有一個建議給你，」青蛙爸爸說，「你不需要選擇，
青蛙在這兩種地方都能過得很好呀。」

August 3

Zip and Kibby and Buffy Squirrel were jumping near Beaver Pond. Tad Frog sat on a rock, watching them.

"What are you doing?" he asked.

"We're having a contest to see who can jump the farthest," said Kibby.

Zip jumped first. He landed on a log near the pond.

茲普、姬碧和松鼠芭菲在「比弗池塘」邊上上下下的跳著，青蛙泰弟坐在一顆石頭上，睜大眼睛看著他們。

「你們在幹什麼?」他問，

「我們在比賽呀，看誰跳得最遠!」姬碧回答。

Kibby jumped next. She landed on the other side of the log.

Buffy jumped last. She jumped all the way to the edge of the pond.

Just then—*zing!*—Tad went flying through the air. He landed on a lily pad in the middle of Beaver Pond.

"Frogs can jump, too," called Tad.

茲普第一個跳，他落在池邊的一根圓木上；

姬碧接著跳，她落在圓木的後面喲；

最後跳的是芭菲，她跳得好遠，跳到了池塘的邊緣呢。

就在那個時候，颼的一聲，泰弟凌空飛越落在「比弗池塘」中央的一片蓮葉上。

「青蛙也能跳喲。」泰弟說。

Zip and Kibby and Buck Beaver stood on the bank of Beaver Pond, waving their arms. Tad hopped over to join them.

"What are you doing?" he asked.

"Buck is teaching us to swim," said Kibby.

"That's right," said Buck. "The first thing you have to do is get used to being in the water."

"I'm used to being in the water," said Tad.

"Then you just paddle with your front legs and kick with your back legs," said Buck. "It's easy."

"Like this?" said Tad, and he hopped into the water and gave a big powerful kick. He came up out of the water on the other side of Beaver Pond.

"I don't think Tad needs any more lessons," said Buck.

茲普、姬碧和河狸巴克站在「比弗池塘」的岸邊上，擺動著他們的雙手，泰弟也跳過去加入他們。

他問：「你們在做什麼啊？」

「巴克在教我們游泳呀。」姬碧回答。

「沒錯，」巴克說，「你們要做的第一件事就是要習慣泡在水裡。」

「我很習慣泡在水裡的。」泰弟說。

「然後你就用前腿划水，後腿踢水，」巴克說，「這很容易的。」

「像這樣子嗎?」泰弟說完就跳進水裡用力踢了一下，等他浮出水面時，已經在「比弗池塘」的另一邊囉!

「我認為泰弟不需要再上什麼課了。」巴克說。

August 5

Kate the butterfly had always known what to do.

When she was a baby caterpillar, she knew that she should wrap herself up in a leaf blanket.

When she was an older caterpillar, she knew that she should eat lots of leaves.

蝴蝶凱特總是知道自己該做什麼。

當她是隻小毛毛蟲時,她知道該把自己裹在一條葉子做的毛毯裡。

當她是隻大毛毛蟲時,她知道自己該吃很多的樹葉。

When she was in danger, she knew that she should hide.

She had even known when the time had come to turn into a butterfly. And later she had known exactly what a butterfly should do.

Now Kate had a startlingly new idea. Something told her to fly back to the bushes where she had lived as a caterpillar.

遇到危險時，她知道要躲起來。

她甚至知道自己什麼時候該變成蝴蝶；變成蝴蝶後，她也很清楚蝴蝶該做些什麼事。

現在凱特有個令人吃驚的新想法。

似乎有某些事物在告訴她，要她回到自己毛毛蟲時期所住過的灌木叢裡去呢。

Kate went back to the bushes—not to eat leaves, but to do something even more important.

She went back to lay eggs.

She laid her eggs on the leaves she liked to eat. Her babies would like those leaves, too. When the little caterpillars hatched, they would have plenty of food nearby.

After she laid her eggs, Kate flew away.

Inside the eggs the baby caterpillars began to grow.

凱特回到了灌木叢裡。她不是來吃葉子，而是做些更重要的事情喔。

原來，她是回到這兒產卵呢。

　　她把卵產在她很愛吃的那種樹葉上，她的寶寶也會喜歡這種葉子的；而且當小毛毛蟲孵化出來後，他們附近就有很充足的食物啦。

　　凱特產下卵以後便飛走了。

　　卵裡面的毛毛蟲寶寶們開始成長囉！

After Kate laid her eggs, she darted about, showing off her colorful butterfly wings. By and by she saw a curiously large brown animal sitting on Snow Hill.

蝴蝶凱特產下卵之後便到處飛舞,炫耀著她那對五彩繽紛的翅膀。

沒多久, 她看到一隻體形奇大無比的棕色動物坐在「雪丘」上。

凱特認為這件事關係重大, 所以便毫無懼色的飛過去, 停在一朵花上。

「先生, 你是誰呀?」她問了,

這隻體形奇大無比的棕色動物驚訝的看見, 竟然有個這麼小的東西這樣稱呼他。

Kate felt very important and not at all afraid. She flew over and sat down on a flower.

"Who are you, Mister?" she asked.

The curiously large brown animal was surprised to see such a tiny creature addressing him.

"Why, I'm Woodsley Bear," he said. "I'm writing a book about Woods Hollow. Who are you?"

"I'm Kate," said Kate. "I know you'll find this hard to believe, but I used to be a caterpillar."

"Well," said Woodsley, "I do know that many strange and wonderful things happen in nature. Your changing from a caterpillar into a butterfly is certainly one of those wonderful things."

"Thank you," said Kate.

「有什麼事嗎？我是大熊伍史利啊！」他說著，「我正在寫一本關於『哈洛小森林』的書。妳又是誰呀？」

「我是凱特，」凱特說，「我知道你可能不會相信，但我以前是隻毛毛蟲喲。」

「這樣啊，」伍史利說話了，「我很清楚大自然裡會發生許多奇怪又美妙的事情。妳從毛毛蟲變成了蝴蝶，必定就是那些美妙事情中的一個呢。」

「謝謝你。」凱特說。

One hot August day Zip and Kibby went to Beaver Pond to see their friend Buck Beaver. Buck was lying on the grass.

"What are you doing today?" asked Zip. "Are you going to make repairs on Beaver Dam? Or plug up leaks in Beaver Lodge? Or cut down some trees?"

"I'm going to rest," said Buck.

"Rest!" cried Zip. "I have never seen you rest."

"I have been working too much," said Buck. "I'm tired."

"You need a vacation," said Kibby.

"What's a vacation?" asked Buck. "I have never heard of that."

在一個炎熱的八月天，茲普和姬碧前往「比弗池塘」拜訪他們的朋友河狸巴克。巴克這時正躺在草地上呢。

「你今天要做些什麼？」茲普問，「你要去修理「比弗水壩」？還是要把「比弗小木屋」漏水的地方塞起來？或是去砍樹？」

「我要休息。」巴克回答。

「休息？」茲普叫了起來，「我從來沒見過你休息呀！」

"A vacation is a long period of time when you do not work," explained Kibby. "You just have fun."

"What a great idea!" said Buck. "I wonder who thought of that?"

「我事情做得太多,」巴克說,「我覺得累了。」

「那你需要個假期。」姬碧說。

「什麼是假期啊?」巴克問,「我從沒聽過這種東西呢。」

「假期就是指你有很長一段時間不用去工作,」姬碧解釋著,「只要玩得開開心心就行了。」

「這主意很棒耶!」巴克說,「是誰想到的點子啊?」

Buck Beaver was packing. He was planning to go away for five days. He was taking a vacation.

"I will get an early start today," said Buck. "As soon as I am packed, I will be on my way."

First he had to think about what he wanted to take with him.

Then he had to find everything.

Next he had to build a big wooden trunk to hold his belongings.

巴克在收拾行李唷，他計畫要去渡五天的假呢。

「我今天要一早出發，」巴克說，「等收拾好行李就上路了。」

首先他得想想要帶些什麼東西，

然後得把東西找齊；

Then he had to build a big wooden wagon
to hold the trunk.

He put his belongings in the trunk. He put
the trunk on the wagon. At last he was ready
to leave.

But he did not get an early start. When he
was finally ready to leave, it was time for bed.

接著，他得釘個大木箱來裝這些東西，

並且再做一個木頭大貨車來放這個大木箱；

最後，他把所有的東西裝進大木箱，再把大木箱搬上貨車。

巴克終於準備好要出發了！

但他並不是一早出發呢，等到他終於要出發的時候，已經是該上
床睡覺的時間囉。

Early in the morning Buck Beaver left
Woods Hollow. He traveled all day. At last he
came to another part of the forest, where
there was a nice pond.

"I think I will spend my vacation here,"
said Buck.

He looked around for a place to sleep.

Near the pond there was an old hollow log.
Buck poked his head inside.

"No vacancy!" cried the rabbit
who lived in the old hollow log.

清晨一早，河狸巴克就離開了「哈洛小森林」。他走了一整天，終
於來到森林的另外一個區域，那兒有個很漂亮的池塘。

「我想，我就在這裡渡假吧！」巴克說著。

他到附近尋找睡覺的地方。

There was a small cave behind some rocks.
Buck peered in at the door.

"No vacancy!" cried the fox who lived in
the small cave.

"I guess I will have to build my own
vacation house," thought Buck.

靠近池塘的地方有個破舊的空心木頭，巴克探頭進去看了看。

「沒有空房間！」住在裡頭的兔子大叫著。

咦！附近的岩石後有個小洞穴呢，巴克從洞穴門邊往裡面瞧一瞧。

「沒有空房間！」住在小洞穴內的狐狸也大叫著。

「看來我得要自己蓋間渡假小屋了。」巴克這樣想著。

Buck Beaver started work on his vacation house.

He spent all morning cutting down trees and gnawing off the branches.

He spent his entire lunchtime hauling the logs and branches to the pond and pushing them into the water.

He spent all afternoon building a dam out of logs and branches and rocks and mud.

8/
11

河狸巴克開始建造他自己的渡假小屋。

他花了整個早上砍下樹木，並把上面的樹枝啃下來；

又花了整個午飯的時間把這些木頭和樹枝拖到池塘，推進池水裡。

巴克花了一個下午用木頭、樹枝、石頭、泥土等建出一個小壩；

He spent the early evening building a
small house near the dam.

He spent the late evening
digging a tunnel from the shore
to his new house.

At last he was finished. And just in time,
too! He was exhausted and ready for bed.

又花整個傍晚在小壩附近蓋了一間小屋；
還花一晚上的時間挖了一條從岸邊到他新屋的地道。
最後，他終於完成了，時間也剛剛好！但巴克累壞了，也準備去
睡囉。

Buck Beaver liked his new vacation house. It had a door and a window. It had a floor and a ceiling.

"But something is missing!" said Buck. "What can it be?"

He decided to eat his breakfast. He looked around for the table.

"Now I know what is missing!" cried Buck. "A table!"

8/
12

河狸巴克挺喜歡他新的渡假小屋。

有門，有窗，還有地板和天花板呢。

「好像還差一些東西，」巴克說著，「會是什麼呢?」

他決定先吃早餐，就四處找桌子。

Buck made a little table out of some extra wood. Now his vacation house had everything.

By this time he was very hungry. But when he sat down at his new table, he landed on the floor.

"Hmmm," said Buck. "Something else is missing. A chair!"

「啊！我知道少了什麼東西了，」巴克叫著，「一張桌子！」

巴克用多餘的木頭做了張小桌子。現在，他的渡假小屋一切東西都有了。

這時巴克肚子餓扁了，就在新桌子前坐了下來，沒想到卻跌到地上。

「嗯……」巴克說，「還少一樣東西呢，一張椅子！」

巴克四處打量著他的渡假小屋，需要的東西都有了呢。

「我這裡有門，可以進進出出，」巴克說，「有窗，可以讓新鮮空氣進來；有地板可以站；有天花板可以擋住炎熱的太陽；有桌子可以吃早餐；還有椅子可以坐呢。」

Buck looked around at his vacation house. He had everything he needed.

"I have a door in case I want to go out or come in," he said. "I have a window to let in the fresh air. I have a floor to stand on. I have a ceiling to protect me from the hot sun. I have a table where I can eat my breakfast. I have a chair to sit on."

Nothing was missing.

Buck decided to have some breakfast. He was very hungry.

He sat down at his new table. He waited and waited. Suddenly it occurred to him that there was something else missing.

Breakfast!

什麼都不缺。

巴克肚子非常餓，他得吃早餐了。

他在新桌子前坐好，等了又等，等了又等；突然間，他才想起來還差一樣東西呢。

早餐呀！

August 14

Buck was still working hard to fix up his vacation house. He made a cupboard for the wall. He filled the cupboard with woodchips and bark and water lilies and other things beavers like to eat.

"There!" he cried. "I'm finished. Now I can relax and enjoy my vacation. No more work for me."

巴克還在努力的整理他的渡假小屋。他在牆上裝了個小櫃子，櫃子裡放滿了木屑、樹皮、睡蓮和其他河狸愛吃的東西。

「好囉!」他叫著，「我做好了。現在我可以輕輕鬆鬆的享受假期，再也沒有任何工作囉!」

Then Buck looked at his calendar.

"Oh, no!" he said. "My work is finished, but so is my vacation. Today is the day I must return to Woods Hollow. Everyone is expecting me."

So Buck packed his trunk. He swept the floor. He closed up the window and locked the door. He started home.

然後，巴克看了看日曆。

「噢，不！」他說，「工作是做完了，但假期也結束了。我今天必須回到『哈洛小森林』，每個人都在等著我呢。」

所以巴克又把行李收進他的木箱子，把地板掃乾淨，關上窗，鎖上門，回家去囉。

茲普和姬碧聽說巴克回家了，便一起去「比弗池塘」看他。

「歡迎回來！」姬碧先說，「假期過得怎麼樣？」

「很棒！」巴克說，「我發現一個很美的池塘，建了一座水壩橫過整個池塘，在水壩的附近蓋了一間房子。我還做了張桌子和椅子來配這間房子，並且把食物收集好。不過，等做好這些事情時，時間也差

When Zip and Kibby heard that Buck was home again, they went over to Beaver Pond to see him.

"Welcome back!" said Kibby. "How was your vacation?"

"Great!" said Buck. "I found a nice pond. I built a dam across the pond. I built a house near the dam. I built a table and chair for the house. I collected food. Then it was time to come home."

"It sounds as if you worked on your vacation," said Zip. "I hope you had fun, too."

"I had fun doing all that work," said Buck. "I guess we beavers just like to work."

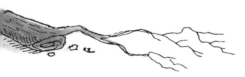

不多該回家了。」

　　「聽起來你整個假期好像都在工作嘛,」茲普說,「我希望你也很開心。」

　　「我是很開心呀,」巴克說,「我想我們河狸就是愛工作吧。」

-------------------------------August 16

On a warm August day in Woods Hollow,
Buffy Squirrel was walking by Stone Ledge.
She felt hot and thirsty. Suddenly she saw a
rock that looked familiar.

"That is one of the rocks where I found
icicles last winter," she thought.

「哈洛小森林」一個暖和的八月天裡，松鼠芭菲經過「大岩崖」
時覺得又熱又渴，突然她看見一塊看上去好熟悉的岩石。

「這不就是我去年冬天找到冰柱的那些岩石之一嗎?」她想著。

The icicles had been cold and wet and pointed at the end. She remembered how she had broken them off and taken them home to Oak Tree. But in the morning the icicles had disappeared. They had all melted.

"I wish there were icicles hanging on that rock now," thought Buffy. "I would break them off and pop them into my mouth. I would call them Ice Pops."

那些冰柱一度又冰又濕，而且尾端還尖尖的；她還記得自己是怎麼把冰柱扭斷，帶回「橡樹」去。可惜到了早上，冰柱通通融掉不見了。

「真希望那些冰柱現在還掛在這岩石上！」芭菲心想，「我就會把它們折下來通通塞到嘴巴裡，把它們叫做『棒棒冰』呢。」

"Tell us a story," said Kibby.

"Once upon a time," said Father Chipmunk, "there was a flower named Gladiolus. Gladiolus liked being a flower. She liked to stand tall. She liked to bask in the sunlight. Most of all she liked to blossom. It made her feel good to open up her petals.

8/17

「給我們說個故事嘛。」姬碧說。

「從前,」花栗鼠爸爸說,「有一朵花叫做唐菖蒲,她很喜歡當一朵花。她喜歡站得直直的,也喜歡曬太陽。更重要的是,她喜歡開著花,打開花瓣的感覺使她好舒服呢。」

"Now, if Gladiolus had had only one blossom on her stem, she could have opened her petals only once. But Gladiolus was lucky. She had many blossoms on her stem. She could open up the petals in each blossom, one after another.

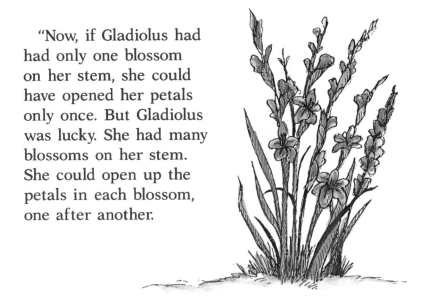

"And that is why," said Father Chipmunk, "gladiolus blossoms never open all at the same time."

The gladiolus is the Flower of the Month for August.

「如果唐菖蒲的花莖上只有一個花苞的話，她就只能開一次的花瓣而已；幸好唐菖蒲很幸運，她的花莖上有好多的花苞，所以就可以一個接一個的打開花瓣呢。」

「這就是為什麼，」花栗鼠爸爸接著說，「唐菖蒲的花苞從不在同時間內全打開的原因唷。」

唐菖蒲是代表八月的花朵

August 18

Toward the end of summer the berries in Woods Hollow were ripe and sweet and delicious. Zip and Kibby filled their baskets with them.

As they picked berries they ate berries. Half of the berries went into the baskets. Half of the berries went into Zip and Kibby.

夏天接近尾聲的時候,「哈洛小森林」的漿果也成熟了,又甜又可口,於是茲普和姬碧把這些漿果裝滿了他們的籃子。

他們邊摘邊吃,邊吃邊摘。摘下的漿果一半放進籃子裡,一半則吃到肚子裡。

花栗鼠媽媽決定在家做漿果醬,茲普和姬碧也幫著把一些鍋子裝

At home Mother Chipmunk decided to make berry jam. Zip and Kibby helped her fill the pots. As they filled pots they ate more berries. Half of the berries went into the pots. Half of the berries went into Zip and Kibby.

Mother Chipmunk cooked the berries and made some jam. When she was finished, she put a bowl of jam on the table for Zip and Kibby to eat with bread.

"We're not hungry," said Zip and Kibby.

"Not hungry!" cried Mother Chipmunk. "I wonder why."

滿漿果，他們邊裝邊吃，邊吃邊裝。漿果有一半裝進了鍋子裡，一半又吃進肚子裡。

花栗鼠媽媽煮熟了那些漿果，把它製成了果醬。等她做好時，她擺了一碗果醬在桌上給茲普和姬碧配著麵包吃。

「我們不餓啊。」茲普和姬碧同時說著，

「不餓！」花栗鼠媽媽叫著，「我倒想知道為什麼喲！」

"Rocky," said Mother Raccoon. "Go and pick some berries so that I can make berry pie. And remember—pick only the sweetest berries!"

Rocky took his pail and went to the berry bushes.

"These berries *look* sweet," thought Rocky. "But how do I know that they really *are* sweet."

He picked a berry and popped it into his mouth.

Yes, that berry was sweet— but now that berry was gone.

「洛奇,」浣熊媽媽說,「去摘些漿果回來,這樣我就可以做漿果派了。記得,只能摘最甜的喲!」

洛奇提起了桶子,往漿果叢裡走去。

「這些漿果看起來很甜呢,」洛奇心想,「但我怎麼知道它們是真的很甜呢?」

He picked another berry
and popped it into his mouth.

That berry was sweet, too—
but now that berry was
also gone.

When Rocky got back home,
Mother Raccoon wondered
why his pail was empty.

"I picked only the sweetest
berries," said Rocky. "But
to be certain they were
all sweet, I had to taste
every single one."

於是，他摘了一顆漿果，「剎」的一聲把它扔進嘴裡。

不錯，這顆很甜──但現在這顆漿果沒了！

他又摘另外一顆，「剎」的一聲把它扔進嘴裡。

這顆也很甜──但現在這顆漿果也沒了！

當洛奇回到家，浣熊媽媽很奇怪為什麼他的桶子是空的。

「我只摘那些最甜的漿果，」洛奇說了，「但是為了確定它們都是
甜的，我只好每一顆都嚐嚐看囉。」

　　姬碧和茲普坐在他們的蘋果樹下，努力想著該怎樣度過這一天。

「我喜歡夏天，」姬碧說，「想想我們在夏天可以做的事多著呢。我們可以去游泳，去健行，還可以到『雪丘』野餐。」

August 20

Kibby and Zip were sitting under their apple tree, trying to decide how to spend the day.

"I love summer," said Kibby. "Just think of all the things we can do in the summer. We can swim. We can hike. We can take a picnic to Snow Hill."

"That's right," said Zip. "We can fish. We can play ball. We can sail a boat on Beaver Pond."

"What shall we do first?" asked Kibby.

They thought and thought, but they did not get up from where they were sitting.

"You know why I *really* love summer?" said Zip. "Because summer is a great time for doing nothing."

「對呀，」茲普也說了，「我們可以釣魚，打球，也可以去「比弗池塘」划船。」

姬碧問：「我們先做什麼好呢?」

他們腦裡不停想著，身體卻也一直坐在那兒沒站起來。

「妳知道為什麼我真的很喜歡夏天嗎?」茲普說，「因為夏天最適合什麼事都不做呢。」

Everyone in Woods Hollow liked Belvedere Owl's weather reports. That was because Belvedere always predicted good weather.

If it was hot, Belvedere always predicted that the weather would get cooler.

One very hot day in Woods Hollow, Belvedere sat at his desk, fanning himself. He looked at his thermometer. He checked his barometer. He consulted all of his charts.

"It looks as if we are going to have some cool, breezy weather," said Belvedere.

Just then a hot blast of air ruffled Belvedere's feathers.

"Pay no attention to the heat," said Belvedere. "I am quite certain the weather is going to be cool tomorrow."

「哈洛小森林」的每一個人都很喜歡貓頭鷹貝弗迪的氣象報告，因為他老是預測會有好天氣。

如果天氣炎熱，貝弗迪總會預測天氣將日漸轉涼。

有一天，「哈洛小森林」特別熱，貝弗迪坐在書桌旁，不停的搧扇子。他看了一下溫度計，查了一下氣壓計，並且把所有的圖表都仔細的研究一番。

「看起來我們將會有涼爽和微風吹拂的天氣喲。」貝弗迪說。

就在這個時候，一陣熱風吹來，弄皺了貝弗迪的羽毛。

「不必在意這暑氣，」貝弗迪說，「我很肯定明天天氣就會轉涼呢。」

August 22

Belvedere Owl sat at his desk, fanning himself
even faster than he had the day before.

He noticed that some of the pine needles on
Tall Pine were turning brown in the heat.

He studied his books. He looked at his maps.
He consulted all of his charts.

"I definitely see cool weather coming our way,"
said Belvedere.

Just then a pile of hot, dry pine needles fell
on Belvedere's head.

貓頭鷹貝弗迪坐在書桌旁，不停的搧著扇子，搧得比昨天還要快
呢。

貝弗迪注意到「大青松」上的一些松針，在太陽的照射下逐漸變
黃。

他把書翻出來研究，把地圖東南西北的看一看，又把圖表仔細的
查閱一番。

"Pay no attention to the heat," said Belvedere.
"I am absolutely sure that the weather is going
to be cool tomorrow."

「我確信觀察到一股涼爽的氣流正朝我們而來。」貝弗迪說著。

就在這個時候，一堆焦黃乾枯的松針落在貝弗迪頭上。

「不必在意這暑氣，」貝弗迪繼續說，「我肯定明天天氣絕對會轉

涼。」

The next day was the hottest day of the year. The flowers drooped. The leaves on the trees drooped. Everyone in Woods Hollow was drooping.

Belvedere Owl went upstairs to his weather station. There was no shade to protect him from the hot sun.

The heat melted the ice in Belvedere's lemonade before he could lift up the glass.

He looked at his thermometer. He checked his barometer. He consulted all of his charts.

隔天是這一年裡最熱的一天。「哈洛小森林」裡花兒憔悴了，葉子枯萎了，就連每個人也都頹喪著。

貓頭鷹貝弗迪爬上他那個沒有陰影可遮陽的氣象臺。

炎熱的高溫在貝弗迪舉起杯子之前，早把檸檬汁裡的冰塊全給溶光了呢。

"I think the weather cannot possibly get any hotter," said Belvedere. "Therefore tomorrow is bound to be cooler."

And this time Belvedere was right.

　　他看了一下溫度計，查了一下氣壓計，又仔細研究他手中所有的圖表。

　　「我看天氣再也不會熱到那裡去了；所以，明天一定會涼爽一些。」貝弗迪說。

　　這一次，貝弗迪可說對了呢！

At the edge of Beaver Pond there was a small, shallow pool. To Zip and Kibby and their friends, it was just a puddle. To Mother and Father Robin, it was a lake.

Mother and Father Robin flew down and landed in the water. They hopped around, and the water splashed up. It splashed on their legs and on their bodies and on their heads.

They began to feel cooler.

Hob, Nob, Bob, and Rob flew down to see what was going on.

「比弗池塘」邊緣有一個淺淺的小水塘。對茲普、姬碧和他們的朋友來說，這只不過是一灘水；但對知更鳥爸爸和媽媽來說，這卻是個湖呢。

知更鳥媽媽和爸爸飛下來，落在這灘水裡。他們到處蹦蹦的跳，

"Come on in!" cried Father Robin. "This lake is big enough for all of us."

And in no time at all there were six robins making splashes instead of two!

水花濺上來，弄得他們從頭到腳都是水呢。

唔，他們開始覺得涼快些了。

荷波、娜波、巴柏和洛柏也飛下來看怎麼回事。

「進來呀！」知更鳥爸爸大叫，「這個湖夠我們所有人玩呢！」

哇！一下子就有六隻知更鳥在水裡拍打水花，而不再只是兩隻囉！

----------------------------- August 25

At high noon on a hot August day, there was not a frog in sight at Beaver Pond.

在一個炎熱的中午,「比弗池塘」裡連一隻青蛙也看不到。

「青蛙都跑到哪去了?」姬碧問著,她正坐在池塘邊的石頭上,兩隻腳泡在水裡。

「我們在這裡。」一個熟悉的聲音說。

姬碧先看看她的右邊,再看看她的左邊,她還是沒有看到任何的青蛙。最後她向下看,哇!有一雙又大又鼓的眼睛就在她的腳邊。

8 / 25

"Where are all the frogs?" asked Kibby as she sat down on a rock and put her feet into the water.

"Here we are," said a familiar voice.

Kibby looked to the right and she looked to the left. She still did not see any frogs. Finally she looked down, and there, next to her feet, were some big bulging eyes.

Tad's eyes.

"This is how we frogs keep cool," explained Tad. "We stay underwater. We keep our eyes *out* of the water just to see what is going on."

"This is how we chipmunks keep cool," said Kibby. "We put our feet *in* the water. We keep the rest of us out of the water just to see what is going on."

那是泰弟的眼睛!

「這就是我們青蛙保持涼爽的方法喔!」泰弟解釋著。「我們待在水底下,只露出兩個眼睛看看外面有什麼動靜就夠了。」

「而我們花栗鼠保持涼爽的方法,」姬碧也說,「則是把腳放在水裡,其他的都露在外面來看看有什麼動靜就夠了。」

　　「山胡桃蜂房」裡一片吵雜，充滿了活力。有些蜜蜂在儲存花蜜，有些在照料蜂蜜，有些則在照顧剛出生的蜜蜂寶寶。

　　在這一個炎熱的八月天，蜂房裡是又忙又熱呢。

Hickory Hive was abuzz with activity. Some of the bees were storing the nectar. Some of the bees were looking after the honey. Some of the bees were taking care of the new baby bees.

On this warm August day the hive was both busy and hot.

But the bees had their own way of keeping cool. They fanned the air with their wings.

Now, if just one bee did this, there would be no breeze at all. If ten bees did this, there would be a little breeze, but not enough to cool the hive. But if a hundred bees fanned—all at the same time—the hive would be a little cooler.

Once again the bees proved the value of their motto—**WORK TOGETHER**.

但蜜蜂有他們自己的方法來保持涼快喔，他們只要用翅膀搧風就行啦。

如果只有一隻蜜蜂這樣做，那是一點風都沒有；如果十隻蜜蜂這麼做，就有一些風出來，但還涼不到整個蜂房；如果一百隻蜜蜂同時搧的話，蜂房就會涼快些了。

在這裡，蜜蜂再一次證明了他們的座右銘——團隊合作——的價值呢。

August 27

One day Buffy put on some green overalls and a big floppy pink hat.

"You look like a flower," said Mother Squirrel. "You have a green stem and a pink flower on top."

8/27

有一天芭菲穿了件綠色的吊帶褲，配上一頂鬆垮垮的粉紅色大軟帽。

「妳看起來像朵花唷，」松鼠媽媽說，「有綠色的花莖，上面還有一朵粉紅色的花。」

芭菲還挺喜歡像朵花呢，所以，她整天都穿著這套花衣裳。

Buffy liked looking like a flower. She wore her flower costume all day.

Later in the afternoon she decided to look for nuts. By and by she came to the hickory tree. She went around and around the trunk of the tree, keeping her eyes turned toward the ground. She was looking for nuts. She did not look up. She did not see what was above her in the hickory tree.

Hickory Hive was up there. And inside the hive was B.G. Bee!

到了下午，芭菲要去找些核果。沒走多久，便來到了山胡桃樹這裡。她在樹幹周圍繞過來又繞過去，眼睛只盯著地上打轉，看看有沒有核果；芭菲並沒有抬頭往上看，所以也就沒看見樹裡有什麼東西。

「山胡桃蜂房」就在那兒，在蜂房裡的正是蜜蜂比姬呢！

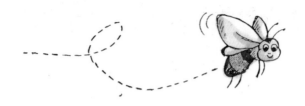

August 28

B.G. Bee decided to go out and look for nectar. She wanted to find the flowers that bloom in the late summer. They would be full of nectar, and she could gather the nectar and take it back to the hive.

She was no sooner out the door of Hickory Hive than she saw something that excited her. It was an enormous flower with a plump green stem and a huge pink blossom.

B.G. flew right up to that enormous flower, buzzing just as busily as could be.

蜜蜂比姬決定到外頭去找花蜜。她想去找些夏末才開的花，這種花的花蜜才多呢，比姬就可以採這些花蜜帶回蜂房。

她一出蜂房的大門，便看到令她興奮的東西——一朵很巨型的花呢，有著粗粗厚厚的綠花莖和粉紅的大花瓣。

比姬就飛向這朵巨型的花，嗡呀嗡的嗡個不停。

Suddenly the flower did something very strange. It ran away. It ran and ran until it disappeared.

B.G. had never before seen a flower that could run so fast. In fact, she had never seen a flower that could run at all.

She wondered if she would ever see it again.

但這朵花突然間做了件不可思議的事，她竟然跑開了！她跑呀跑呀，一下子就跑得無影無蹤。

比姬從沒有看過哪朵花能跑得那麼快！事實上，她從沒有看過花會跑呢！

比姬不知道會不會再看到這朵花。

---------------------------- August 29

Zip and Kibby decided to play ball.

Zip threw the ball to Kibby. She swung at
the ball with her bat. The bat missed the
ball, and the ball rolled down the path.

"We need someone to catch the ball," said
Kibby.

茲普和姬碧決定打棒球。

茲普把球投給姬碧，姬碧揮棒落空，球滾落在地上。

「我們需要有人來接球。」姬碧說了。

正好芭菲剛走過來，他們便要她做捕手。

茲普再投球，這一次姬碧擊中了球，趕緊跑向一壘。茲普把球投
向一壘，但一壘上並沒有人可以刺殺姬碧。

「要找個人當一壘手才行。」茲普說。

Just then Buffy came along. They made her the catcher.

Zip threw the ball again. This time Kibby hit the ball and ran to first base. Zip threw the ball to first base, but no one was there to tag Kibby.

"We need someone to play first base," said Zip.

Then Rocky came along. They made him first baseman.

Zip threw the ball again. This time Kibby hit the ball so hard that it went right over Zip's head. It landed far away.

"That's a fly ball!" cried Zip. "We need someone to catch flies."

Tad jumped up.

"I'm good at catching flies," he said.

洛奇正好走過來，他們便要他做一壘手。

茲普再投球，這一次姬碧用力的擊中球心，球飛過茲普的頭上，落到很遠的地方。

「這是個高飛球呢！」茲普叫著，「我們需要找個人來接高飛球。」

泰弟跳了起來。

「我最擅長接高飛球了。」他說。

-------------------------------- August 30

Zip and Kibby and their friends were playing ball. It was Buffy's turn at bat.

"I don't know how to hit the ball," said Buffy, holding the bat.

"Just watch the ball," said Zip.

"Swing hard," said Kibby.

Zip threw the ball to Buffy. Buffy kept her eyes on the ball. When it got close to her, she swung hard.

Whack! The ball sailed into the air and landed out of sight.

茲普、姬碧和他們的朋友在打棒球，現在輪到芭菲打擊。

芭菲手中拿著球棒說著：「我不知道怎麼打到球啊？」

茲普說：「看著球就行了。」

「用力揮棒。」姬碧也說。

Buffy ran to first base, second base, third base. Still no one had found the ball. So she ran to home base.

"I guess I know how to hit the ball now," said Buffy.

"I guess you know how to make a home run now, too," said Kibby.

茲普把球投向芭菲，芭菲緊緊盯著那個球，等球靠近時，她把球棒用力一揮。

鏗的一聲，球飛到空中，落在視線以外。

芭菲跑到一壘，二壘，跑到三壘了！還是沒有人找到球，所以她就跑回了本壘。

「我想我現在知道怎麼打球了。」芭菲說。

「我想妳也知道怎麼擊出全壘打囉！」姬碧回答著。

Summer was coming to an end. The warm days would soon grow cooler. The long days would soon grow shorter.

Zip and Kibby were sitting with their father in the shade of their favorite apple tree.

"I wish it could be summer forever," said Zip.

"If it were always summer," said Father Chipmunk, "there would be no fall, winter, or spring."

"We would miss Halloween in the fall," said Kibby.

"We would miss Christmas in the winter," said Buffy.

"We would miss Easter in the spring," said Rocky.

夏天就要結束了，悶熱的日子也快要逐漸轉涼囉。

長長的白天也快要變短了。

茲普、姬碧和他們的父親坐在他們喜愛的蘋果樹的樹蔭底下。

茲普說：「我希望永遠都是夏天。」

「假如永遠都是夏天，」花栗鼠爸爸說，「那就會沒有秋天、冬天

"Each season is different and wonderful in a special way," said Father Chipmunk.

"I guess I would not like to miss any of them," said Zip.

和春天囉。」

　　「我們會錯過在秋天的萬聖節。」姬碧說。

　　「我們會錯過在冬天的聖誕節。」芭菲也說。

　　「我們會錯過在春天的復活節。」洛奇接著說。

　　花栗鼠爸爸告訴大家：「每一個季節都有它特殊和可愛的地方。」

　　「我想我不會喜歡錯過其中的任何一個呢。」茲普說。

LABOR DAY

　　茲普和姬碧到處在找巴克，他們預料找到巴克時，他一定在忙著工作。但相反的，他們卻發現巴克躺在地上休息，什麼事也沒做。

　　「怎麼了?」姬碧問了，「你受傷了? 還是生病了?」

　　「我很好呀!」巴克回答著，「今天是勞動節。」

September 1

Zip and Kibby were looking for Buck. They expected to find him working, but instead they found him lying on the ground, doing nothing.

"What's wrong?" said Kibby. "Are you hurt? Are you sick?"

"I'm fine," said Buck. "Today is Labor Day."

"What is Labor Day?" asked Zip.

"Labor Day is the day we honor everyone who works," explained Buck. "I'm someone who works, so Labor Day is a special day for me. It always comes on the first Monday in September, because Monday is usually a working day. On Labor Day, Monday is a holiday."

"That's the best way to honor workers," said Kibby. "Give them a day off."

「什麼是勞動節啊?」茲普問,

「勞動節是我們向每一位勞工致敬的日子,」巴克解釋著,「我也是位勞工, 所以勞動節對我來說是很特別的日子。勞動節總是在九月的第一個星期一, 因為星期一通常都要工作;但是在勞動節的星期一則是個假日唷。」

「嗯, 讓勞工放假一天是向勞工致敬的最好方法了。」姬碧這麼說著。

Mother Raccoon, who was the school teacher at Woods Hollow School, did not work during summer vacation. But in September she went back to work.

Did Mother Raccoon go back to work on the first day of school? No! She went back to work *before* the first day of school.

She had to get ready for her students.

Before the first day of school, Mother Raccoon cleaned the schoolroom, dusted the tables and shelves, and put pictures up on the walls.

浣熊媽媽是「哈洛小森林學校」的老師。浣熊媽媽在暑假裡是不用工作的，但到了九月，她便得回學校工作了。

浣熊媽媽是在開學的第一天才回學校的嗎？錯了，浣熊媽媽在開學前就要開始工作囉。

她得為學生準備好一切。

She wrote names on
coat hooks and new books.

She mixed paint
and made clay.

She took out the paste
and the scissors and
the blocks and the puzzles.

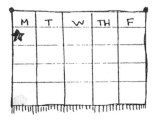

She made charts and
wrote stories and planned
interesting things to do.

Before the first day of school, Mother
Raccoon was very busy.

開學前，浣熊媽媽把教室打掃乾淨，把桌上和架子上的灰塵擦掉，
把畫掛好；
她把學生的名字一一寫在掛大衣的衣鉤上和新書裡；
也把顏料調好、黏土準備好；
她還要把漿糊、剪刀、積木和拼圖等東西拿出來擺好；
再把各種圖表畫好，寫一些故事和準備很多有趣的教材。
浣熊媽媽在學校開學前非常忙碌呢！

浣熊爸爸是「哈洛小森林」的森林管理員。在夏季結束的時候，他必須特別提高警覺，因為森林在夏季受了太多日曬，雨量又少，所以樹木這時都會變得很乾燥，隨時都有發生火災的危險。

大火會毀掉整座森林。如果真是這樣子，大家就再也無法住在「哈洛小森林」裡了。

Father Raccoon, as forester of Woods Hollow, had to be especially alert at the end of the summer. The forest was dry because there had been so much sunshine and so little rain. There was always a danger of fire.

Fire could destroy the entire forest. And if it did, no one could live in Woods Hollow anymore.

Father Raccoon had important work to do. His work helped everybody feel safe.

Every day he looked for signs of fire. He did not just look for fire. He looked for smoke. A little smoke could turn into a big fire.

Father Raccoon did his work well. There were no dangerous fires in Woods Hollow. Everyone was very careful.

因此，浣熊爸爸的工作就非常重要，他的工作讓每個人都覺得很安全。

他每一天都要四處找尋任何會起火的跡象。他不僅要注意火苗，也要注意煙，一點點的煙也可能變成一場大火呢。

浣熊爸爸把他的工作做得非常好，「哈洛小森林」從沒發生過任何危險的火災。

每個人也都非常小心呢。

Mother Squirrel was the mail carrier in Woods Hollow. As mail carrier, she had to know where all the mailboxes were located. But knowing *where* they were was not enough. She had to be able to get to them. Some mailboxes were easy to reach.

Belvedere Owl's mailbox was conveniently located at the base of Tall Pine.

The Chipmunk family's mailbox stood just outside the door to their burrow.

9 / 4

松鼠媽媽是「哈洛小森林」的郵差。身為郵差，松鼠媽媽就必須知道所有的信箱在什麼地方；光知道還不夠，她也必須能到那裡才行。

有些信箱很容易就能到達。

貓頭鷹貝弗迪的信箱設的很方便，就在「大青松」的樹底下。

花栗鼠家的信箱就在他們洞穴的門外。

The Raccoon family's mailbox was next to their log.

Buck Beaver's mailbox was also next to his house, but his house happened to be in the middle of Beaver Pond. In the winter Mother Squirrel could walk across the ice to deliver the mail to Buck. But during the rest of the year she had to swim or use a boat.

浣熊家的信箱也在他們圓木小屋的旁邊。

河貍巴克家的信箱也一樣在屋子的旁邊，但他的家恰巧是在「比弗池塘」的中央。冬天時，松鼠媽媽還可以走過冰面送信給巴克，但其他的日子裡，她只好以游泳或划船的方式送信囉。

"Mother," said Buffy Squirrel. "Why did you decide to be a mail carrier? Why did you choose that job?"

Mother Squirrel put a loaf of acorn bread into the oven to bake.

"When I was little," said Mother Squirrel, "I liked to collect things."

"I like to collect things," said Buffy.

"I collected nuts, leaves, pine cones, and pebbles," said Mother Squirrel. "I collected twigs, paper, string, and paper bags."

"*I* collect those things, too," said Buffy.

"So when I grew up," said Mother Squirrel, "I decided to collect the mail."

"We are a lot alike, Mother," said Buffy. "Maybe *I* will collect the mail when I grow up."

「媽，」芭菲問著，「妳為什麼決定當郵差呢？為什麼會選這份工作？」

松鼠媽媽正把一條堅果麵包放進烤箱裡烤。

「我小的時候，」她回答著，「喜歡收集東西。」

「我也喜歡收集東西呀。」芭菲說。

「我收集核果、樹葉、松果、小石頭，」松鼠媽媽又說，「還有樹枝、紙張、細線和紙袋。」

芭菲接著說：「我也收集這些東西呢。」

「所以我長大的時候，」松鼠媽媽把話說完，「就決定收集信件。」

「媽，我們有很多地方很相像呢，」芭菲說了，「我長大後或許也會收集信件唷。」

September 6

On or around Labor Day, Belvedere Owl paused to think about the importance of his job.

"Without a weather owl," thought Belvedere, "there would be no . . . weather!"

Belvedere chuckled. That, of course, was not true.

"Without a weather owl," Belvedere began again, "there would be no . . . *good* weather!"

Belvedere chuckled again. Even *that* was not true.

勞動節前後，貓頭鷹貝弗迪停下來想著他那份工作的重要性。

「沒有了預報氣象的貓頭鷹，」他心裡想著，「那就沒有……天氣了！」

貝弗迪想到這，忍不住笑了起來，因為這當然不會是真的。

「沒有了預報氣象的貓頭鷹，」他又開始想，「那就沒有……好天氣了！」

Weather reporters did not make weather, and they did not control the weather.

"I know," thought Belvedere. "Without a weather owl, there would be no weather reports. Everyone would wonder: Is it going to rain today? Is it going to snow?"

Belvedere Owl's job was certainly an important one!

貝弗迪又吃吃的笑起來，因為就連他預報的天氣也不全是真的呢。

氣象播報員既不會製造天氣，也無法控制天氣呀。

「啊，我知道了！」貝弗迪想到，「沒有了預報氣象的貓頭鷹，那就沒有氣象報告。這樣的話，每個人都會懷疑今天會不會下雨？會不會下雪？」

看來，貝弗迪的工作確實是很重要唷！

----------September 7

The bees who lived in Hickory Hive had different jobs. B.G. Bee wondered which job was most important.

Certain bees took care of the baby bees. If they did not do this, the baby bees would not grow up and take care of the hive.

Other bees collected the nectar from flowers. If they did not do this, there would be no nectar for making the honey.

「山胡桃蜂房」裡的蜜蜂都有不同的工作，蜜蜂比姬很想知道哪一樣工作是最重要的。

某些蜜蜂負責照顧蜜蜂寶寶。如果這些蜜蜂不這麼做，蜜蜂寶寶就會長不大，也就無法看管蜂房了。

有些蜜蜂負責採集花蜜。如果他們不做這工作，那就沒有花蜜來做蜂蜜了。

Still other bees made the honey. If they did not do this, there would be no honey to feed the baby bees, and they would not grow up and take care of the hive.

But the bees who collected the nectar had to know where to find it. Bees like B.G. had to go out and find the nectar. Without nectar there would be no honey. Without honey there would be no food for baby bees.

So it seemed to B.G. that her job—scout bee—was the most important one.

還有些蜜蜂負責製造蜂蜜。如果他們不這樣做，就沒有蜂蜜來餵蜜蜂寶寶，蜜蜂寶寶就長不大，也就沒有辦法看管蜂房呢。

但採集花蜜的蜜蜂必須知道要到哪裡去採呀，所以像比姬這種蜜蜂就必須出外去找花蜜。沒有花蜜，就沒有蜂蜜；沒有蜂蜜，蜜蜂寶寶就沒有食物了。

因此對比姬來說，她這偵察蜂的工作是最重要的喲。

----------------------- September 8

On the first day of school ten little beavers carried ten little lunch boxes from Beaver Lodge to Woods Hollow School. At school they hung their ten little sweaters on ten little hooks and looked around the room to see what they could do.

One little beaver sat in the book corner— and looked at books.

Two little beavers sat in the art corner— and drew pictures.

　　開學的第一天，十隻小河貍帶了十個小小的午餐盒，從「比弗小木屋」到「哈洛小森林學校」上課去。到了學校，他們先把十件小毛衣掛在小掛鉤上，然後在教室四處看看有什麼事可以做。

Three little beavers stayed in the clay corner—and made things out of clay.

Four little beavers went to the block corner—and made things out of blocks.

One, plus two, plus three, plus four—that took care of ten little beavers, as well as all four corners in the Woods Hollow schoolhouse.

一隻小河狸坐在放書的角落看書了；

兩隻小河狸坐在放畫的角落畫畫了；

三隻小河狸待在放黏土的角落，用黏土捏出各種東西；

四隻小河狸待在放積木的角落，用積木堆出各種東西；

一加二加三加四──嗯，這樣的組合把十隻小河狸和教室的四個

角落分配得剛剛好呢！

"Today," said Mother Raccoon, the teacher at Woods Hollow School, "we are going to make jam. Think of a kind of jam you would like to make."

在「哈洛小森林」裡，浣熊媽媽對著學生說，「我們今天要來做JAM。想一想，你們要做哪一種JAM呀?」

姬碧說：「我要做草莓JAM。」

茲普也說：「我想做藍莓JAM。」

浣熊媽媽走過去看看十隻小河狸在做些什麼，她發現他們正在玩一些玩具小圓木。小河狸們把小圓木堆成一堆，有些擺向這邊，有些

"I would like to make strawberry jam," said Kibby.

"I would like to make blueberry jam," said Zip.

Mother Raccoon went to see what the ten little beavers were doing. She found them playing with some toy logs. They were piling the toy logs together—this way and that way —so that the logs stuck out in all directions.

"What kind of jam would *you* like to make?" asked Mother Raccoon.

"We have already made our jam," said the ten little beavers, pointing to the pile of toy logs. "It's a *log*jam, just right for starting a beaver dam!"

擺向那邊，使得小圓木各自往不同的方向伸出去。

浣熊媽媽問了：「你們想做哪一種JAM啊?」

「我們把JAM做好了呀!」十隻小河狸指著這堆玩具小圓木回答，「這是個圓木JAM，拿來蓋個河狸水壩挺合適的呢!」

【譯者註：JAM有兩種解釋，一為果醬，一為阻塞堆積之物。此篇故事利用英文特有的雙關語來營造一種俏皮的氣氛；浣熊媽媽指的是果醬的JAM，而小河狸指的卻是堆積物的JAM。】

September 10

Mother Raccoon was teaching her pupils about their neighborhood.

浣熊媽媽正在教學生們了解附近的環境。

「『哈洛小森林』最高的地方是在哪裡呀?」浣熊媽媽問了,

姬碧回答:「最高的地方就是『雪丘』頂啊。」

「『哈洛小森林』最低的地方是在哪裡呢?」浣熊媽媽又問,

"What is the highest place in Woods Hollow?" asked Mother Raccoon.

"The top of Snow Hill is the highest place," said Kibby.

"What is the lowest place in Woods Hollow?" asked Mother Raccoon.

"The bottom of Beaver Pond is the lowest place," said Zip.

"And which place is closest?" asked Mother Raccoon.

"I know!" cried Rocky. "Woods Hollow School! We are right *in* it."

茲普回答:「最低的地方就是『比弗池塘』的池底呀。」

「最近的地方又是哪裡呢?」浣熊媽媽再問,

「我知道!」洛奇大聲的說,「是『哈洛小森林學校』! 我們就在這裡面呀。」

September 11

Beaver Dam was an underwater wall which went across one end of Beaver Pond. The dam kept the water from flowing out, making the pond bigger and deeper.

One day Buck discovered a leak in the dam. He decided to fix it.

First he had to collect small branches. He dragged each branch along the ground and through the water. He tucked each branch into the hole in the dam.

「比弗水壩」就像是水底下的一面牆,橫過了「比弗池塘」的一端。它擋住了池水使它不外流,好讓池塘變得更深更大。

有一天,巴克發現水壩有一個小裂縫,決定把它修好。

首先,他得收集些小樹枝,然後一根一根的拖過地面,游過池水,把樹枝一一的塞進裂縫裡。

Next he had to collect small rocks. He carried the rocks to the pond and through the water. He tucked the rocks into the spaces between the branches.

Finally he had to collect mud. He brought the mud up from the bottom of the pond. He used the mud to hold the branches and rocks in place.

接下來，他要收集小石頭。他把石頭一顆顆的運到池塘，游過池水，把石頭塞進樹枝間的縫隙。

最後，巴克得收集泥巴。他把泥巴從池底挖上來，用泥巴把樹枝和石頭固定起來。

While Buck was repairing Beaver Dam, his ten brothers and sisters played nearby. They were pretending to be dam builders.

當巴克在修理「比弗水壩」時，他的十個弟弟妹妹也在附近玩耍，把自己當成是那些建築水壩的工程人員呢。

小河狸們就在一條從「比弗池塘」流出的小溪上面，建造一座橫越小溪的水壩。

他們先在小溪上堆滿了大大小小的樹枝，小溪流經過這些樹枝時就得慢慢、慢慢的流了。

A small creek flowed out from one end of Beaver Pond. The little beavers were building a dam across the creek.

First they piled up twigs. The water flowed more slowly past the twigs.

Then they tucked pebbles into the spaces between the twigs. The water became just a trickle.

Finally they put bits of mud here and there. The water stopped flowing at all. A little pool was growing behind the dam.

Buck came to see the little dam.

"Even when beavers play, they work," he said.

　　然後，他們用些小圓石塞住樹枝之間的縫隙，流過這些樹枝的溪水便只能一滴一滴的流了。

　　最後，他們在樹枝外面，這裡一點、那裡一點的塗上泥巴；這樣子，水就完全流不出來，水壩的後面也就逐漸形成一個小水塘了。

　　巴克來看這個小水壩時說著：「嘻嘻，河狸在遊戲的時候也不忘工作呢。」

September 13

"Tell us a story," said Zip.

"Once upon a time," said Father Chipmunk, "there was a delicate blue flower without a name. The blue flower was so fragile that she had to wrap herself around other nearby objects to support herself as she grew.

「說個故事給我們聽呀。」茲普說。

「從前呢，」花栗鼠爸爸說了，「有一朵姿態很優雅的藍花，但是她卻沒有名字。這朵藍花非常的脆弱，她生長時必須把自己纏在別的東西上才能支撐住。」

「雖然這朵藍花很喜歡開得大大的，但她無法承受太多的日光，又因為下午的陽光太熱太強，所以她只在早上開花。每個清晨時分，

"Even though the blue flower loved to grow, she could not stand too much sun. Because the afternoon sunshine was much too hot and bright, the flower blossomed only in the morning. She opened her blue petals as wide as she could during the early hours and closed them tightly at noon.

"And that is how," said Father Chipmunk, "the blue flower got her name—Morning Glory!"

The morning glory is the Flower of the Month for September.

她儘可能的把藍色的花瓣開得大大的，一到中午便緊緊的合起花瓣。」

「也因為這樣，這朵藍花就被人稱做morning glory（牽牛花）了。」花栗鼠爸爸說著。

牽牛花是代表九月的花朵

【譯者註：morning glory的英文花名直譯為「早晨的榮耀」，中文名稱則是「牽牛花」。】

Hob, Nob, Bob, and Rob went to visit Belvedere Owl.

"How do you get to be a weatherman? . . . I mean weather owl?" asked Hob.

"You have to know all about weather," said Belvedere.

荷波、娜波、巴柏和洛柏一起去拜訪貓頭鷹貝弗迪。

「你是怎麼成為一位氣象播報人員的? ……我是指成為一位報氣象的貓頭鷹?」荷波問。

貝弗迪回答:「你們必須知道所有關於天氣的事情。」

「我們知道所有天氣的事情呀,」娜波說話了,「天氣有時候冷,有時候熱;有時候濕濕的,有時候又不會。還有什麼必須知道的呢?」

"We know all about weather," said Nob. "Sometimes it's cold and sometimes it's hot. Sometimes it's wet and sometimes it's not. What else do you have to know?"

"You have to know about clouds," said Belvedere.

"We know about clouds," said Bob. "Clouds are in the sky. Nobody knows why. What else do you have to know?"

"You have to know the different *kinds* of weather," said Belvedere.

"That's easy," said Rob. "There's good weather and there's bad weather. What else do you have to know?"

Belvedere sighed. It was going to be a long afternoon.

貝弗迪回答：「雲囉，你們一定得了解雲。」

「我們很清楚雲呀，」巴柏也說，「雲就是在天空中嘛，沒人知道為什麼。還有什麼是必須知道的呢？」

貝弗迪回答：「你們還必須知道各種不同的天氣。」

「那簡單，」洛柏說，「天氣有好的天氣和壞的天氣。還有什麼是一定要知道的？」

貝弗迪重重的嘆了口氣，這會是個很長很長的下午囉！

September 15

Belvedere Owl was teaching Hob, Nob, Bob, and Rob about the weather.

"It's important to know the right names for things," Belvedere explained. "For example, what do you call little drops of water that fall out of the sky?"

"Rain," answered Hob.
"Wrong," said Belvedere. "We weather owls call them *precipitation*."

貓頭鷹貝弗迪正在教荷波、娜波、巴柏和洛柏關於天氣的情形。

「有一點很重要，就是要知道各種東西的正確名稱。」貝弗迪解釋著，「例如，你們怎麼稱呼從天上掉下來的水滴呢？」

「雨呀。」荷波回答著。

「錯啦，」貝弗迪說，「我們氣象播報貓頭鷹會稱這些水滴為『液

"Then, what do you call those dark clouds in the sky?" asked Nob, noticing some dark clouds overhead. "Do you call them precipitation clouds?"

"No," said Belvedere. "We call them *nimbostratus* clouds."

Suddenly big drops of rain began to fall. "I think," said Bob, looking for shelter, "that one of those nimbostratuses is precipitating."

態降水』。」

　　「這樣的話，那你怎麼稱呼天上的黑雲呢?」娜波注意到她頭頂上的烏雲，便這樣問著，「你是不是就叫它『液態降水雲』呢?」

　　「不，」貝弗迪說，「我們稱它為『雨層雲』……」

　　突然間，大顆大顆的雨點開始落了下來。

　　「我想，」巴柏邊找躲雨的地方邊說著，「某一朵『雨層雲』正在『液態降水』囉。」

September 16

It was raining in Woods Hollow. Zip and Kibby opened up their big umbrella and stood under it. Although rain was falling all around them, they stayed dry.

Buffy came scampering along, her fur dripping.

"Come under our umbrella, Buffy," said Zip. And Buffy did.

Rocky came hurrying by, splashing in the puddles.

"Come under our umbrella, Rocky," said Zip. And Rocky did.

While they were standing under the big umbrella with the rain falling all around them, they saw Tad. Tad was hopping about, as wet as a frog could be.

「哈洛小森林」正下著雨。茲普和姬碧撐開了他們那把大雨傘，站在傘底下。雖然在他們四周的雨一直下著，他們全身還是乾爽的呢。

芭菲急急忙忙向他們跑過來，身上的毛都滴著水呢。

「芭菲，到我們的傘底下來。」茲普說著。芭菲就跑進傘底下來。

"Come under our umbrella, Tad," said Zip.
But Tad did not.

"No, thanks!" cried Tad. "Frogs never mind
the rain. Frogs love to get wet."

洛奇匆匆忙忙的經過他們附近，弄得水花四濺。

「洛奇，到我們的傘底下來。」茲普說著。洛奇也就跑進傘底下。

雨還是在四周不停下著，他們也就一直在傘底下站著。這個時候，
他們看見了泰弟。泰弟到處蹦蹦跳跳著，全身都濕透了。

「泰弟，到我們的傘底下來。」茲普又說著，但泰弟並沒有這樣做。

「不用啦，謝謝你！」泰弟大叫，「青蛙才不在意雨呢！我們喜歡
弄得濕濕的。」

伴隨九月而來的不只是清涼的微風，還有著一份全新的心情呢。
茲普和姬碧感受了那份心情，覺得該把一切事情做得妥妥當當。

「我們來整理櫥櫃吧。」茲普說。

說完，他們就馬上動手工作。茲普搬開玩具時，發現了一個空盒
子；姬碧則在收拾衣服時，發現了一堆拼圖。

September 17

September brought with it cool breezes and a new feeling. Zip and Kibby had that new feeling. They wanted to get things done.

"Let's clean our closet," said Zip.

They went right to work. Zip moved some toys and found an empty box. Kibby picked up some clothes and found a pile of puzzle pieces.

"Here is the box for the puzzle with five hundred pieces," said Zip.

"And here are the five hundred pieces," said Kibby.

As they picked up the pieces and put them into the box, they talked about the puzzle.

"It was fun doing this puzzle," said Kibby.

"Let's do it again," said Zip.

And so they did.

「嘿，這裡有裝那五百片拼圖的盒子呢。」茲普說。

「那五百片的拼圖就在這裡呀。」姬碧回答。

他們兩個一邊撿起一片片的拼圖放回盒裡去，一邊談論著這些拼圖。

姬碧說：「這些拼圖玩起來很有趣呢。」

「那就再玩一次吧！」茲普說。

結果，他們又玩了起來。

Buffy watched her friends Kibby and Zip working on their puzzle.

"It's going to be a picture of Woods Hollow in the summertime," said Zip. "Would you like to help us?"

"I don't know how to do puzzles," said Buffy. "I'll just watch."

Zip put pieces of the sky together. He found all the blue pieces but one.

"Here's the missing piece," said Buffy, and she handed him a white piece. "There's a white cloud in the blue sky."

Kibby put pieces of the grass together. She found all the green pieces but one.

"Here's the missing piece," said Buffy, and she handed Kibby a gray piece. "There's a gray rock in the green grass."

---

9 / 18

芭菲看著她兩位朋友姬碧和茲普在玩拼圖。

「唔，這會是一張『哈洛小森林』夏天的圖案呢，」茲普說,「妳要不要幫我們一點忙?」

「我不會玩拼圖,」芭菲說,「我看著就好了。」

茲普要把「天空」那部分的拼圖組合起來,他找到了所有藍色的拼圖片,就是找不到最後一片。

"The biggest puzzle to me," said Zip, "is
why Buffy always thinks she doesn't know
how to do anything."

　　「這就是找不到的那一片，」芭菲說著，然後遞給茲普一片白色的
拼圖片，「藍色的天空要配一朵白色的雲。」

　　姬碧要把「草地」那部分的拼圖組合起來，她找到了所有綠色的
拼圖片，但是就差最後一片。

　　「這就是找不到的那一片，」芭菲說著，然後拿給姬碧一片灰色的
拼圖片。「綠色的草地要配一塊灰色的石頭。」

　　「我最想不通的就是，」茲普說，「為什麼芭菲老是認為她什麼都
不會呢？」

Grandpa Ground Hog was the dentist in Woods Hollow.

Every September, Buck Beaver took his ten brothers and sisters to see Grandpa Ground Hog. He liked to catch Grandpa Ground Hog before he went to sleep for the winter. Grandpa Ground Hog had a way of sleeping at least until February.

Grandpa Ground Hog looked at each little beaver's teeth. He checked them and cleaned them and counted them. He counted teeth *and* he counted beavers.

"I have checked ten little beavers' teeth," he said at last. "Does that mean that I have checked everybody?"

9/19

土撥鼠老爹是「哈洛小森林」的牙醫。

每年九月，河狸巴克都會帶著他的十個弟弟妹妹去看土撥鼠老爹。他總是喜歡在土撥鼠老爹冬眠前趕去找他，因為土撥鼠老爹冬眠時，一睡最少能睡到隔年的二月。

"Yes," said Buck. "I have ten brothers and sisters, and you have checked ten sets of teeth. That means that you have checked everybody."

But Buck was wrong. Which beaver had not had his teeth checked by Grandpa Ground Hog?

土撥鼠老爹看了每隻小河狸的牙齒。他仔細的一一檢查，清洗清洗，還數一數有幾顆牙齒；同時也數了河狸的數目。

「我已經檢查過十隻河狸的牙齒囉。」他最後說了。

「這是不是表示每一個人都檢查過了呀？」

「沒錯」巴克說，「我有十個弟弟妹妹，你也檢查了十副牙齒，那就是說你每一位都檢查過了。」

但巴克弄錯了喲！是哪一隻河狸還沒被土撥鼠老爹檢查牙齒呢？

It was time for Buck Beaver to have *his* teeth checked and cleaned. He sat down in Grandpa Ground Hog's special chair. The chair went up for short patients and down for tall patients. Grandpa Ground Hog put the chair down for Buck.

First he looked at the front teeth. Then he looked at the back teeth. He used his little mirror to see every part of every tooth.

"Your teeth are very healthy," said Grandpa Ground Hog.

"I have healthy teeth because I·brush them carefully and eat good foods," explained Buck.

"And," said Grandpa Ground Hog, peering at Buck's two front teeth, "your two front teeth are so-o-o sharp. How do you keep them that way?"

現在該河狸巴克去檢查和清洗他自己的牙齒了。他坐上了土撥鼠老爹那張特製的椅子，這張椅子可以調高給個子矮的病人坐，也可以調低給個子高的病人坐。土撥鼠老爹替巴克把椅子調低一點。

他首先檢查巴克前面的牙齒，再來是後面的牙齒。土撥鼠老爹還用一支小鏡子來察看牙齒的每個部位。

"It's easy if you're a beaver," answered Buck. "I sharpen my teeth by using them to chop down trees."

「你的牙齒很健康唷!」土撥鼠老爹說了。

「我的牙齒很健康是因為我刷牙很仔細,而且還吃好的東西。」巴克解釋。

「還有,」土撥鼠老爹盯著巴克的兩顆門牙說,「你的兩顆門牙真的非常尖耶,你是如何維持的呢?」

「如果你是隻河貍的話,就很簡單了,」巴克回答,「我常用牙齒把樹木啃下來,所以牙齒磨得很利呀。」

今天是夏季的最後一天。「大岩崖」附近的一片灌木葉上，有些蝴蝶卵開始要孵化囉，但從這些卵裡出來的不是蝴蝶，而是一條一條綠色的小毛毛蟲喲。

那些都是凱特的孩子呢！

這些毛毛蟲在葉子上扭扭擺擺的動了一陣以後，便各自分頭出發了。

On the last day of summer some butterfly eggs began to hatch on a leaf in a bush near Stone Ledge. Out of those eggs came—not butterflies, but small green caterpillars.

Kate's children!

The caterpillars wiggled around on the leaf for a while. Then they all set off in different directions.

The weather was no longer warm. The leaves were no longer fresh. They were beginning to curl and sag.

Kate's children knew just what to do. They rolled themselves up in leaf blankets and went to sleep.

They would not wake up until spring.

　　這時的氣候不再是那麼暖和，樹葉也不再那麼鮮嫩，甚至還開始捲起來往下垂呢。

　　凱特的孩子倒知道該怎麼做。他們把自己裹在一張毛毯般的葉子裡，乖乖的睡覺去。

　　他們要一直睡到春天才會醒唷。

September 22

One morning Belvedere Owl announced
that it was the first day of autumn. No one
was surprised.

"I could tell it was autumn," said Zip,
"because some of the leaves are changing color."

"I knew autumn was here," said Kibby,
"because the weather is cooler."

　　有一天早上，貓頭鷹貝弗迪宣布當天就是秋季的第一天，但沒有
任何人感到驚訝。

　　「我看得出來秋天已經到了，」茲普說，「因為有些樹葉都在變顏
色了。」

"It feels like autumn to me," said Buffy, "because school has started. But Belvedere, you are an official weather expert. You must have a real reason for knowing that autumn has come. Is it something in the sky? Is it something in the air? Is it something on the ground?"

"No," said Belvedere, preparing to fly back to Tall Pine. "It is something I read in a book."

「我早知道秋天已經到了，」姬碧也說，「因為天氣比較涼了。」

「我也感覺秋天到了，」芭菲說，「因為學校開學了呀。但貝弗迪，你是公認的氣象專家，一定有很正確的理由知道秋天已經到了吧。是因為天空中的某些現象？或者是因為空氣中的某些現象？還是地面上的現象呢？」

「都不是，」正準備飛回「大青松」的貝弗迪回答說，「我是從書裡讀到的。」

Buffy Squirrel was hunting for acorns near Stone Ledge when she saw Rocky Raccoon.

"Isn't it wonderful?" she cried. "Autumn is here. Autumn is my very favorite season. In the autumn there are acorns and pine cones and lots of nuts."

松鼠芭菲在「大岩崖」附近找堅果的時候，看到了浣熊洛奇。

「這不是很棒嗎?」她大叫著，「秋天來了呢。秋天是我最喜愛的季節了，會有好多堅果、松果和核果呢!」

「秋季是我最喜愛的季節了，」洛奇說，「在秋季，有紅的、黃的和橘色的葉子呢!」

"Fall is *my* favorite season," said Rocky. "In the fall there are red and yellow and orange leaves."

"Autumn is best, though," said Buffy.

"No, fall is best," said Rocky.

Just then Buck Beaver came by.

"This sounds like a silly argument," said Buck. "You know, you are arguing about the same season. Sometimes it's called autumn and some-times it's called fall, but— whichever name you use— it's the same season."

芭菲說:「但秋天是最棒的喲。」

「不，秋季才是最棒的。」洛奇說。

這時，河狸巴克恰巧經過這裡。

「這聽起來像個很傻的爭論呢,」巴克說, 「你們知道嗎? 你們爭論的是同一個季節! 我們有時候叫它秋天, 有時候叫做秋季; 但不管用什麼名字, 都是同一個季節呢。」

September 24

Now that autumn had come to Woods Hollow, everyone began to notice changes. The changes were signs of the new season.

"There are nuts and seeds on the ground," said Zip.

9 / 24

秋天已經降臨「哈洛小森林」了，每個人開始留意到一些變化，這些變化也正是新季節來臨的跡象呢。

「地上到處都是核果和種子呢。」茲普說。

He shivered. The air was chilly.

"The apples are ripe," said Kibby. She shivered, too. "Brrrr. I'm cold."

"I'm cold, too," said Zip. "We should get our sweaters. Our sweaters will keep us warm."

"That is another sign of autumn," said Kibby. "It's time to wear sweaters again."

他的身體顫了一下，因為天氣涼颼颼的哪。

「蘋果也熟了唷，」姬碧說著也抖了一下，「唔，好冷哦。」

「我也覺得好冷，」茲普說，「我們該拿件毛衣，毛衣會保暖呢。」

「對了，這也是秋天的另外一種跡象哦，」姬碧說，「又到了該穿毛衣的時候啦。」

It was bedtime at Beaver Lodge. Ten little beavers were climbing into ten little beds.

"Look out the window," said one little beaver. "It's dark outside. When we went to bed in the summer, it was still light outside."

"Hooray!" shouted ten little beavers. "Buck is letting us go to bed later. Buck has changed our bedtime."

"No," said Buck. "You are not going to bed later. You are going to bed at the same time. In the fall the days are shorter and the darkness comes sooner. It is not your bedtime that has changed. It is the season that has changed."

「比弗小木屋」裡就寢的時間到了，十隻小河狸紛紛爬上十張小床。

「嘿，看窗外！外面都黑了呢，」一隻小河狸說，「夏天上床睡覺的時候，天還好亮呢。」

「好耶！」十隻小河狸叫著，「巴克讓我們晚一點上床睡囉！巴克改了我們睡覺的時間囉！」

「不，」巴克說，「你們並沒有晚睡，你們上床睡覺的時間還是一樣的。只不過秋天的時候，白天比較短，天黑的比較快而已。你們就寢的時間沒有變，而是季節變了。」

"Everyone has been looking for signs of autumn," Buffy told her mother, "and I cannot find any."

"Where did you look?" asked Mother Squirrel.

"I have been too busy to look for signs of autumn," said Buffy. "I have been busy hunting for nuts and other things. And if I am not hunting, I am busy *collecting* nuts and other things. And if I am not collecting, I am busy *sorting* nuts and other things. I have sorted all the things I have collected into many different piles."

"Did you know that autumn is the time of year when squirrels feel most like hunting and collecting and sorting?" said Mother Squirrel. "That means that one good sign of autumn is a busy squirrel named Buffy."

9
/
26

「每個人都在找秋天的跡象，」芭菲告訴她媽媽，「但我什麼都找不到呢。」

松鼠媽媽問：「妳都到哪裡去找呢？」

「我忙得都沒有時間去找秋天的跡象，」芭菲說，「我一直忙著去找核果和別的東西呀。如果不是在找核果，就是忙著去收集核果和別

的東西；如果不是去收集這些，就是忙著把核果和別的東西分開放。
我已經把所有東西都分類完畢，一堆堆的放好喲。」

「妳知道嗎？秋天是松鼠們一年之中最想去找東西，去收集東西
以及把東西分門別類的時候呢。」松鼠媽媽說，「也就是說，秋天來臨
的最好跡象就是一隻叫芭菲的忙碌松鼠呢。」

在一個涼爽的九月天，茲普和姬碧爬到蘋果樹上四處瞧瞧，他們發覺在樹上有很多東西可看唷。

September 27

One cool September day Zip and Kibby climbed up into the apple tree to have a look around. They found plenty of things to see up there.

Apples!

Dozens of apples were hanging from every branch—red and ripe and ready to eat.

Zip and Kibby each picked an apple and ate it. The apples were sweet and juicy inside.

"Isn't it amazing?" said Kibby. "In every apple there are apple seeds."

"And in every apple seed," said Zip, "there's a new apple tree just waiting to begin."

就是蘋果呀!

成打的蘋果懸在樹枝上,紅咚咚、熟透透的,都可以吃了呢。

茲普和姬碧各自摘了一個蘋果來嚐嚐。嗯……裡面又甜又多汁。

「這不是很神奇嗎?」姬碧說,「每一顆蘋果裡都有蘋果的種子。」

「而且每一顆蘋果種子裡面,又都有一顆新的蘋果樹等著要萌芽呢!」茲普也說。

One September day when the sun was
shining but the air was cool, Rocky Raccoon
stood with his father next to the apple tree.
Father Raccoon was holding a large basket.
Rocky was holding a small one.

"When the big basket
is full of apples,"
said Father Raccoon,
"we will make something
special."

九月的某一天，太陽高高照著，但天氣還是涼颼颼的。浣熊洛奇
和爸爸站在蘋果樹旁，浣熊爸爸手中提著一個大桶子，洛奇則提著一
個小桶子。

「等大桶子裝滿蘋果的時候，」浣熊爸爸說，「我們就拿去做些特
別的東西。」

洛奇爬到樹上去摘蘋果。他摘了蘋果就放進小桶子裡交給爸爸，

Rocky climbed up into the apple tree. He picked some apples and put them into his little basket. He handed the little basket to his father. Father Raccoon emptied the little basket into the big basket.

"Is the big basket full yet, Dad?" asked Rocky.

"Not yet, son," said Father Raccoon.

Rocky filled the little basket again and again and again. Each time Father Raccoon emptied it into the big basket.

"Is the big basket full yet, Dad?" asked Rocky.

At last his father answered yes. Rocky was done picking apples.

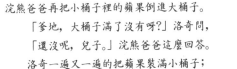

浣熊爸爸再把小桶子裡的蘋果倒進大桶子。

「爹地，大桶子滿了沒有呀?」洛奇問，

「還沒呢，兒子。」浣熊爸爸這麼回答。

洛奇一遍又一遍的把蘋果裝滿小桶子；

浣熊爸爸一次又一次的把蘋果通通倒進大桶子裡。

「爹地，大桶子滿了沒有呀?」洛奇再問，

浣熊爸爸終於說聲「好了」，洛奇才算完成了摘蘋果的任務。

Father Raccoon cut up the apples that Rocky had picked. He put them into a big pan. The pan had tiny holes in the bottom. He put another pan a few inches below the one with the holes in it.

Rocky was very curious. "We are making something with apples," he said. "But what can it be? Is it apple pie? Is it apple cake? Is it apple jelly?"

"No, we are not making any of those things," said Father Raccoon.

He placed a heavy weight on top of the apple pieces. The weight pressed the apples down.

Drip, drip, drip!

Rocky looked to see what was dripping.

浣熊爸爸把洛奇摘回來的蘋果切成一片片，然後放在一個底部有許多小孔的大平底鍋裡，又在大平底鍋下面隔了幾吋的地方，墊上另外一個平底鍋。

洛奇非常的好奇，「我們要用蘋果做些東西耶，」他說了，「但會是什麼呢？蘋果派？蘋果蛋糕？還是蘋果凍？」

Juice was dripping through the tiny holes in the bottom of the pan. The second pan was catching it.

Rocky put his finger between the two pans and caught a drop. He tasted it.

"I know what it is!" cried Rocky. "We are making apple juice."

「不，我們並不是在做這些東西。」浣熊爸爸回答。

他在那些蘋果片上壓了一個很重的東西，蘋果都被壓的扁扁的。

滴，滴，滴……

洛奇仔細看著滴下來的東西。

一些汁液正從大平底鍋底部的小孔中滴出來，下面的平底鍋則接住了這些汁液。

洛奇伸了根手指頭，在兩個鍋子中間接了一滴果汁來嚐一嚐。

「我知道是什麼了！」洛奇叫著，「我們在做蘋果汁！」

河狸巴克帶了一些蘋果給在「比弗小木屋」的弟弟妹妹們。當他把蘋果數一數之後，卻發現只有九個！他一定是弄丟了一個。

巴克十個弟弟妹妹們都盯著巴克，看看他會怎麼辦。每個人都在懷疑——自己會不會是沒分到蘋果的那一個？

Buck Beaver brought some apples to his brothers and sisters at Beaver Lodge. But when he counted them, he discovered that he had only nine apples. He must have dropped one!

All ten of Buck's brothers and sisters were watching to see what Buck would do. Each one wondered—will I be the one who doesn't get an apple?

"It's easy to divide nine apples among ten little beavers," said Buck, "if you make applesauce."

He cut up the apples and put them in a pot. He cooked the apples over the fire. Soon they were soft and saucy.

The pan was full of applesauce. Buck spooned the applesauce into ten little cups.

There was just enough for everyone!

「要把九個蘋果分給十個小河狸是很容易的呀,」巴克這麼說著,「只要做成蘋果醬就成了。」

於是他把蘋果切碎,放進一個鍋子裡;再用火一煮,沒多久蘋果便變得軟的,看起來很好吃呢。

巴克用湯匙把一鍋子的蘋果醬舀入十個小杯子裡;

剛好夠給十隻小河狸呢!

　　十月的第一天，大熊伍史利找荷波、娜波、巴柏和洛柏聊一

聊。

　　「告訴我，荷波、娜波、巴柏、洛柏，」大熊伍史利說了，「你們

彼此誰是誰啊?」

On the first day of October, Woodsley Bear talked to Hob, Nob, Bob, and Rob.

"Now, tell me, Hob, Nob, Bob, and Rob," said Woodsley Bear. "Who is who?"

"It's easy to tell us apart," answered Hob. "For instance, I'm the athletic one."

"And I'm very artistic," said Nob. "Can't you tell?"

"I'm intellectual," said Bob. "You should always be able to tell which one I am."

"And I'm the social one," said Rob. "We are all just as different as can be."

Woodsley Bear stared at the four little robins for a long time. They all still looked alike to him.

「我們很容易分辨的呀，」荷波回答說，「譬如說，我是最愛運動的。」

「我是最有藝術細胞的，」娜波說，「你看不出來嗎？」

「我是很聰明的那一個，」巴柏說，「你應該看得出來我是哪一個吧。」

「我則是社交型的，」洛柏說，「我們根本都不一樣啊。」

大熊伍史利盯著這四隻小知更鳥看了好久好久，在他的眼中，他們看起來還是一個模樣。

On the second day of October, Woodsley Bear talked to Mother Frog.

"Now, tell me, Mother Frog," said Woodsley Bear. "How many eggs did you lay?"

"Nine hundred and ninety-eight," answered Mother Frog.

"Didn't you feel like telling everyone you saw?" asked Woodsley.

"Well, I may have told a few friends," said Mother Frog. "But I *never* brag."

十月的第二天，大熊伍史利和青蛙媽媽聊了一會兒。

「嗯，青蛙媽媽，告訴我，」大熊伍史利說，「妳下了多少顆蛋?」

「九百九十八顆。」青蛙媽媽回答。

"Well, I think that you are very special," said Woodsley, "and I am going to tell about you in my book."

"A book! A book!" cried Mother Frog. "I'm going to be in a book? . . . Wait until I tell Mother Duck about this!"

「妳有沒有想過要告訴每個遇見的人這件事呢?」伍史利又問。

「這個嘛,我可能有說給一些朋友聽啦,」青蛙媽媽說,「但我從不吹牛喔。」

「嗯,我覺得妳很特別,我要在我的書裡談到妳。」伍史利說。

「書! 一本書!」青蛙媽媽嚷起來,「我要被寫在一本書上? 哇! ……先等我告訴鴨媽媽這件事吧!」

On the third day of October, Woodsley Bear talked to Belvedere Owl. Because Belvedere Owl worked at the top of Tall Pine, Woodsley remembered to bring a ladder. He wanted to see the weather station with his own eyes.

十月的第三天，大熊伍史利和貓頭鷹貝弗迪也聊了一會。

因為貝弗迪是在「大青松」頂端工作，所以伍史利也記得帶把梯子來，他想親眼瞧瞧氣象臺。

He asked Belvedere to tell him about the equipment he kept in the weather station.

"Well," said Belvedere proudly. "I have maps, charts, books, and pictures. I have thermometers and barometers. I have an instrument to check the speed of wind and a weather vane to tell me which direction it's coming from."

"I see," said Woodsley. "Then after you check your equipment, you are able to *scientifically* predict what the weather will be."

"Not at all," said Belvedere. "I just guess."

他請貝弗迪解釋氣象臺裡的儀器給他聽。

「好呀！」貝弗迪得意洋洋的說，「我有地圖、圖表、書籍、圖片，溫度計和氣壓計我也有。我還有個儀器用來測量風速的呢，以及一個風向標來告訴我風從哪個方向來哨。」

「我懂了，」伍史利說，「那你在查看這些儀器之後，便能夠很科學地預測天氣會怎樣了哦。」

「才不呢，」貝弗迪回答了，「我是用猜的。」

October 4

On the fourth day of October, Woodsley Bear talked to Buffy Squirrel.

"What do you like to do?" Woodsley asked her.

"I like to collect things," said Buffy.

"What do you like to collect?" asked Woodsley.

"I like to collect nuts," said Buffy. "I collect all kinds of nuts—acorns, chestnuts, walnuts. I used to collect hickory nuts, but I don't anymore."

十月的第四天，大熊伍史利和松鼠芭菲聊天。

「妳喜歡做些什麼事呀？」伍史利問她。

「我喜歡收集各種東西。」芭菲說。

「妳喜歡收集什麼呢？」伍史利問。

"Why did you stop collecting hickory nuts?"
asked Woodsley Bear.

"Once I went to the hickory tree to collect
hickory nuts," said Buffy, "and a scary thing
happened. A bee came right up to me. It
was buzzing and acting very interested in
my hat. In fact, it tried to land on my hat. I
ran away and never went back."

「核果呀，」芭菲說，「各式各樣的核果，像是堅果啦、栗果啦、
胡桃等。我以前也收集山胡桃，但現在沒有了。」

「妳為什麼不再收集山胡桃了呢?」大熊伍史利問。

「我有一次到山胡桃樹去收集山胡桃，」芭菲說，「發生了一件好
可怕的事呢。一隻蜜蜂嗡嗡嗡的向我直飛過來，她對我那頂帽子非常
有興趣；事實上呀，她是想落到我的帽子上呢。我拔腿就跑，從此再
也不去那裡了。」

On the fifth day of October, Woodsley Bear went to see B.G. Bee.

"Now, tell me, B.G.," said Woodsley Bear, "what is your job at Hickory Hive?"

"My job is to find the flowers," said B.G. "I'm a scout bee."

"Have you seen any interesting flowers lately?" asked Woodsley.

"Yes, indeed," answered B.G. "Not too long ago I saw a giant flower. It had a pink blossom and a green stem and two arms and two legs and a bushy tail."

"Hmmmm," said Woodsley. "I have never heard of a flower with arms and legs and a bushy tail. However, I have heard of *squirrels* with bushy tails. In fact, a squirrel has arms and legs *and* a bushy tail."

十月的第五天，大熊伍史利去拜訪蜜蜂比姬。

「來，告訴我，比姬，」大熊伍史利說，「妳在『山胡桃蜂房』的工作是什麼呢?」

「到處去找花呀，」比姬說，「我是隻偵察蜂。」

「妳最近有沒有看到什麼有趣的花朵啊?」伍史利問。

"I have never heard of a squirrel," said B.G. Bee.

　　「有啊！是有這麼一回事。」比姬回答，「不久以前，我看到了一朵很大很大的花。它有粉紅色的花瓣，綠色的花莖，兩隻手臂，兩條腿，還有一個毛茸茸的尾巴！」

　　「嗯……」伍史利說，「我從來沒有聽過花有手臂、雙腿和毛茸茸的尾巴。不過，我倒是聽過松鼠有毛茸茸的尾巴。事實上，松鼠是有兩隻手和兩條腿，還有一條毛茸茸的尾巴唷。」

　　「我從來沒聽過松鼠這種東西呢。」蜜蜂比姬說。

On the sixth day of October, Woodsley Bear went to see Buffy Squirrel again.

"What were you wearing when you went to the hickory tree to collect hickory nuts?" asked Woodsley Bear.

"I was wearing green overalls and a big floppy pink hat," said Buffy. "My mother said I looked just like a flower."

"I thought so," said Woodsley. "Put on your flower costume again and come with me."

Buffy put on the green overalls and the pink hat and went with Woodsley Bear to the hickory tree.

B.G. Bee was flying up to the hive when she saw Buffy.

"Help! Help!" she cried. "It's the giant flower!"

十月的第六天，大熊伍史利再次的拜訪松鼠芭菲。

「妳去山胡桃樹收集山胡桃時，是穿什麼衣服去的?」大熊伍史利問。

「我穿了件綠色的吊帶裝呀，戴了一頂軟軟的粉紅色大帽子，」芭菲說，「我媽還說我像朵花呢!」

「我想也是，」伍史利又說，「妳再穿上妳那套花衣裳跟我來。」

芭菲便穿上那件綠色的吊帶裝和粉紅色的帽子，和大熊伍史利去了山胡桃樹那兒。

"This is not a giant flower." Woodsley laughed. "This is a little squirrel named Buffy."
And that was how Buffy met B.G. After their meeting, Buffy was no longer afraid to look for hickory nuts. Whenever she did, B.G. always came out of the hive to say hello.

蜜蜂比姬正要飛回蜂房時，看見了芭菲便大叫：「救命呀！救命呀！就是這朵大花唷！」

「這不是一朵大花，」伍史利笑著說，「這是隻小松鼠，叫做芭菲。」

這就是芭菲遇見比姬的經過。這一次會面以後，芭菲再也不怕去找尋山胡桃了；每次她去的時候，比姬都會從蜂房裡飛出來跟她打聲招呼呢。

"Tell us a story," said Zip.

"Once upon a time," said Father Chipmunk, "there was a flower known as Calendula. Now, Calendula was not the prettiest flower in the garden. And Calendula did not have the most delightful fragrance. Even her color—yellow-orange—was common. Yet she was one of the gardener's favorite flowers.

"When the rain came, it did not bother Calendula. When the wind blew, it did not bother Calendula. When the sun was hot, it did not bother Calendula. She was strong. She grew well and blossomed in all kinds of weather.

"And that is why," said Father Chipmunk, "the calendula has always been a favorite with gardeners. It is so easy to grow."

「說個故事給我們聽嘛。」茲普說。

「從前,」花栗鼠爸爸說,「有一朵花叫做金盞花。她不是花園裡最漂亮的花,也沒有很迷人的香味,甚至她橘黃的花瓣顏色也很普通。然而,她卻是園丁心目中最喜愛的花朵之一。」

「下雨、刮風、烈日曝曬都難不倒金盞花。她的生命力很強,在任何的天氣裡都能長得很好。」

10/7

The calendula is the Flower of the Month for October.

「這也是為什麼，」花栗鼠爸爸說，「金盞花總是園丁心目中所喜愛的花朵之一。因為，她很容易就生長喔。」

金盞花是代表十月的花朵

Buffy gazed at the branches of Oak Tree. They were covered with bright-yellow leaves.

"It is nice living in Oak Tree in the fall," said Buffy. "Yellow is Oak Tree's *fall* color."

"Fall colors are everywhere," said Mother Squirrel. "Just look around you."

Buffy did look. She saw orange flowers and dark green mosses. She saw brown nuts, brown pine cones, brown leaves. There were even some purple grapes.

She saw yellow corn and yellow squashes. She saw red apples, red berries, red leaves. There were even some golden dandelions.

Mother Squirrel was right. In the fall Woods Hollow was a very special place.

芭菲睜大眼睛的打量著「橡樹」的枝椏，樹枝上已經布滿了鮮黃的樹葉呢。

「秋天時，住在「橡樹」好舒服喲，」芭菲說，「黃色是「橡樹」秋天時的顏色呢。」

「秋天的顏色到處都有，」松鼠媽媽說，「看看妳的四周呀。」

芭菲看著四周，映入眼簾的是一片橘色的鮮花及深綠色的苔蘚；

也有棕色的核果和褐色的松果，還配著咖啡色的葉子；甚至還有些紫色的葡萄哨。

　　她也看見了黃色的玉米、黃色的南瓜、紅色的蘋果、紅色的莓子、紅色的樹葉，甚至還看到些金黃色的蒲公英呢！

　　松鼠媽媽說的對，秋天的「哈洛小森林」真是個別緻的地方呢。

Buck Beaver was preparing for winter.

He had to be certain that Beaver Lodge was cozy and warm so that he and his sisters and brothers would be comfortable there all winter. Beaver Lodge would protect them from the rain and the wind and the snow.

Buck checked the front door and then he swam around to check the back door. Both doors to the lodge were underwater.

Next he gathered food. He had to be certain that he and his brothers and sisters would have enough to eat for many months. During the winter it was hard to find food.

He used part of Beaver Lodge as a storeroom. He piled up bark and twigs and leaves and roots—all the things that beavers like to eat.

河狸巴克在準備過冬了。

巴克必須確定「比弗小木屋」很舒適而且很暖和。這樣的話,他的弟弟妹妹才能過一個舒舒服服的冬天,因為「比弗小木屋」會保護他們不受風雨和大雪的侵襲呢。

巴克先檢查了前門,再轉身游到後門去檢查,小屋的兩扇門都是在水底下的呢!

Especially woodchips!
There was nothing
better on a cold winter's
night than a bowl of
hot woodchip soup.

接下來，巴克要收集食物。他要確定在未來的幾個月內，弟弟妹妹們都有足夠的東西吃，因為在冬天裡是很難找到食物的。

巴克把一部分的「比弗小木屋」當做貯藏室，堆上一些樹皮、樹枝、樹葉和樹根等，這些都是河狸愛吃的東西。

尤其是那些木屑！

在寒冬的夜晚，沒有什麼比來上一碗木屑熱湯更好的了。

October 10

Mother Squirrel was preparing for winter, too. First she collected many dry leaves. These she used to line their home in Oak Tree. The leaves would keep the house warm.

松鼠媽媽也在準備過冬了。

她先去撿了很多的乾葉子用來鋪在「橡樹」的家裡,使房子暖和。

「我撿樹葉是把它當作遊戲,」芭菲說,「我從不知道樹葉這麼有用呢。」

"When I play," said Buffy, "I collect leaves. But I didn't know that leaves could be so useful."

Next Mother Squirrel collected twigs. These she used to plug up the holes in Oak Tree. The twigs would keep out the wind and snow.

"When I play," said Buffy, "I collect twigs. But I didn't know that twigs could be so useful."

Then Mother Squirrel collected nuts and seeds. These she hid in different places around Oak Tree. The nuts and seeds would be their food all winter.

"What do you know!" cried Buffy. "All this time I have been collecting things squirrels really need."

"When you were playing," said Mother Squirrel, "you were also learning to be a good squirrel."

接下來，松鼠媽媽再去收集小樹枝，用來塞住「橡樹」上的那些小洞；如此一來，風雪都吹不進來囉。

「我撿小樹枝是把它當作遊戲，」芭菲說，「我從不知道樹枝也這麼有用呢。」

然後，松鼠媽媽再去收集些核果和種子。她要把這些東西藏在「橡樹」的各個角落，這些核果和種子就是他們整個冬天的食物唷。

「真想不到呀！」芭菲嚷著，「我這些日子所撿的東西竟會是松鼠們真正需要的呢！」

「妳在遊戲的時候，」松鼠媽媽說了，「其實也就是在學習做一隻好松鼠呢。」

Mother and Father Raccoon were also preparing for winter.

One day Mother Raccoon collected nuts. She stored the nuts in big baskets. But several days later she noticed that some of the baskets were empty.

"Someone has been eating the nuts," said Mother Raccoon.

Another day Father Raccoon collected berries. He stored the berries in large jars. But several days later he noticed that some of the jars were empty.

"Someone has been eating the berries," said Father Raccoon.

Mother and Father Raccoon noticed that someone named Rocky was getting fatter and fatter.

浣熊爸爸和浣熊媽媽也在準備過冬呢。

有一天，浣熊媽媽撿了些核果存在幾個大籃子裡；但幾天後，她注意有好多籃子都是空空的呢。

「唔，有人在吃這些核果唷。」浣熊媽媽說著。

"I am the someone who has been eating nuts and berries," Rocky admitted. "I am helping to store food. You are storing food inside baskets and jars. I am storing food inside *me*."

另外有一天，浣熊爸爸也撿了些漿果存在幾個大瓶子裡；但幾天後，他注意到有好多瓶子都是空空的呢。

「唔，有人在吃這些漿果唷。」浣熊爸爸說。

浣熊媽媽和浣熊爸爸也注意到有個叫洛奇的人愈來愈胖了呢。

「我就是那個吃了漿果和核果的人啦，」洛奇承認，「我也在幫忙把食物存起來呀。你們是把食物存在籃子和瓶子裡；我是把食物藏在我的肚子裡。」

Kibby and Zip went to see Buck Beaver.
Buck looked different. He was wearing a
short black cape and a hat with a feather in it.

"Why are you wearing those clothes?"
asked Kibby.

"This is the way Christopher Columbus
dressed when he discovered America,"
explained Buck. "Today is his birthday."

"Tell us about him," said Zip.

"Christopher Columbus lived a long time ago,
when most people thought that the earth was
flat," explained Buck. "But Columbus believed
that the earth was round. He was a very
good sailor. He loved the water."

Buck stopped and looked out at Beaver Pond.
"So do I," he added happily.

姬碧和茲普一起去探望河狸巴克，巴克看起來很不一樣唷！他披
了一件黑色短披風，戴著一頂有羽毛的帽子。

「你為什麼穿這樣的衣服呢？」姬碧問。

「哥倫布發現美洲大陸的時候，就是這樣的穿著呢，」巴克解釋，

「今天是他的生日。」

「說些他的故事給我們聽吧。」茲普說。

「哥倫布是很久以前的人。那個時候，大多數的人都認為地球是平的，」巴克解釋，「但哥倫布相信地球是圓的。他是一個非常棒的水手，而且熱愛『水』。」

巴克說到這停了下來，注視著「比弗池塘」，

「我也是一樣很愛水唷！」他很高興的補上這麼一句。

October 13

Belvedere Owl sat at his desk at the top of
Tall Pine, thinking about clouds.

貓頭鷹貝弗迪坐在「大青松」樹頂的書桌前，想著關於雲的種種。

「想到雲總是會讓我昏昏欲睡，」貝弗迪說，「上一次試著要記下
它們的名字，結果卻睡著了。這一次我一定要保持清醒。」

他把那本關於雲的大書拿出來，開始讀了起來；每種雲都有它自
己的名字，所以有很多不同的名字要記呢。

10/
13

"Thinking about clouds always makes me sleepy," said Belvedere. "The last time I tried to memorize their names, I fell asleep. This time I must stay awake."

He took out his big book about clouds and began to read it. Each kind of cloud had its own name, and there were so many different names to remember!

"There are cirrus clouds and cumulus clouds," said Belvedere. "There are cirrostratus and cumulostratus . . . And then there are . . . "

Belvedere began to yawn.

"There are . . . " Belvedere went on slowly, "cumulonimbus and nimbo . . . stratus and . . ."

But Belvedere never got to the next name. He had fallen asleep again.

「有卷雲，有積雲，」貝弗迪唸著，「有卷層雲、層積雲……然後……有……」

貝弗迪開始打起呵欠來了！

「有……」貝弗迪的速度慢了下來，「積雨雲和雨雲……層雲……」

貝弗迪永遠不會唸到下一個名字了，

因為他又睡著了呀！

Mother Frog was sitting on a rock on the bank of Beaver Pond when Mother Duck and her seven ducklings walked by.

"What a nice family you have!" said Mother Frog.

"Thank you," replied Mother Duck. "I don't see your nine hundred and ninety-eight children with you. How are they doing?"

"I guess they are fine," said Mother Frog. "They don't follow me around the way your children do."

10/
14

當鴨媽媽和她七隻小鴨走過的時候，青蛙媽媽正蹲坐在「比弗池塘」旁的一塊石頭上。

「妳有很可愛的家庭呢。」青蛙媽媽說。

"That is probably just as well," said Mother Duck. "It is not always easy to be followed by seven children. I cannot imagine what it would be like to be followed by nine hundred and ninety-eight!"

「謝謝，」鴨媽媽回答著，「咦？我沒看到妳那九百九十八個小孩和妳在一塊，他們現在怎麼樣啦？」

「我想還好吧，」青蛙媽媽回答，「他們不會像妳的孩子跟著妳一樣，跟我到處跑。」

「那或許也不錯唷，」鴨媽媽說，「有七個小孩跟著並不是很好應付的。我沒法想像九百九十八個孩子跟在後面會是什麼樣的情形呢？」

Mother Raccoon was teaching her pupils at Woods Hollow School about north, south, east, and west.

"If you walked west from the school, where would you be?" she asked.

"You would be at Oak Tree," said Buffy.

"If you walked east from the school, where would you be?" asked Mother Raccoon.

"You would be at Hickory Tree," said Zip.

"If you walked south from school, where would you be?" asked Mother Raccoon.

"You would be at Zip and Kibby's house," said Rocky.

"And if you walked north from the school, where would you be?" asked Mother Raccoon, who knew that the answer was Beaver Pond.

"I know!" cried Kibby. "You would be up to your neck in water."

10/15

浣熊媽媽在「哈洛小森林學校」教她的學生認識東、南、西、北。

她問:「假如你從學校往西走,會走到哪裡去呢?」

「會走到『橡樹』呀。」芭菲回答了。

她問：「假如你從學校往東走，會走到哪裡去呢？」

「會走到『山胡桃樹』呀。」茲普回答了。

她又問：「假如你從學校往南走，會走到哪裡去呢？」

「會到茲普和姬碧的家呀。」這一次洛奇回答了。

她再問：「假如你從學校往北走，會走到哪裡去呢？」浣熊媽媽知道答案應是「比弗池塘」。

「我知道！」姬碧叫著，「會被水淹到脖子上呢。」

------------------------------October 16

During the fall many things fell out of the trees when the wind blew. Things that had been growing on the trees all summer came down to the ground.

Leaves fell—oak leaves, maple leaves. They floated and fluttered on their way down.

Pine cones fell. They just dropped down. They were too heavy to float.

在秋天裡，許多東西被風一吹便紛紛從樹上掉落，儘管它們整個夏季長得好好的，這時還是掉到地上來。

樹葉落了。橡樹葉、楓葉等都飄飄浮浮的落下來。

松果掉了。它們就只是筆直的掉下來，因為它們實在重得飄不起來。

Seed pods blew out of maple trees. Apples fell out of apple trees. Seed pods, apples, and pine cones—*all* of these things had seeds in them.

Nuts fell, too—acorns, walnuts, and hickory nuts. All of these nuts contained seeds, too.

The seeds had a reason for coming down to the ground. Do you know what it was?

種子莢從楓樹上爆開了，蘋果從樹上掉落了，它們裡頭都帶有種子哨。

核果也掉落了。堅果、胡桃、山胡桃等也都帶有種子呢。

種子落到地面來是有原因的哨，你知道是什麼嗎？

One October day Father Raccoon went to visit Belvedere Owl at Tall Pine. He was just about to call up to Belvedere when he noticed a tiny pine tree growing nearby.

Father Raccoon was always interested in trees—especially new trees—because he was the forester in Woods Hollow.

The tiny pine tree looked like Tall Pine, although it was much, much smaller.

Belvedere Owl flew down to say hello to Father Raccoon.

"I want you to meet your new neighbor," said Father Raccoon.

"Who is that?" asked Belvedere, looking around.

"His name," said Father Raccoon, pointing down to the little tree, "is Short Pine."

十月裡的某一天，浣熊爸爸到「大青松」那兒去拜訪貓頭鷹貝弗迪。他正要喊在樹上的貝弗迪時，注意到附近長了一棵小松樹。

浣熊爸爸是「哈洛小森林」的森林管理員，所以一向對樹木很感興趣，尤其是那些剛長出的小樹。

儘管這棵小松樹長得這麼細小，他看起來非常像「大青松」唷。

10/
17

這時，貝弗迪飛下來和浣熊爸爸打招呼。

「來見見你的新鄰居吧。」浣熊爸爸說著。

貝弗迪看一看四周，問了：「誰啊?」

「他的名字，」浣熊爸爸指著地上的那棵小樹說，「就叫『小矮松』呢。」

High above the ground Belvedere Owl sat in his weather station doing his weather work. Far below, a little tree named Short Pine was doing something, too. It was growing.

A year ago a pine cone had fallen out of Tall Pine. It had landed on the ground in a soft, wet place. The seeds in the pine cone had fallen out and had become buried in the soil.

　　貓頭鷹貝弗迪坐在他位於高處的氣象臺裡，忙著他的氣象工作。老遠的樹底下，有棵叫「小矮松」的小松樹也在忙呢，他正在成長唷！

　　一年前，一顆松果自「大青松」裡掉了下來，落在一塊鬆軟潮濕的地方；松果內的種子也掉出來被埋在土裡。

Then came the winter and the little pine tree seeds slept under the ground. In the spring, when the ground was warmer, one little seed sprouted and began to grow. It poked its way out of the ground and went right on growing.

Short Pine was growing, but it grew slowly. It would take Short Pine many, many years to grow as tall as Tall Pine.

然後冬天來臨了，這些小小的松果種子就睡在地底下。到了春天，大地比較暖和的時候，一顆種子萌芽，開始生長了；他鑽出地面，邁向成長之路。

「小矮松」在成長著，但速度很慢；他得花上好多好多年才能和「大青松」一樣高呢。

一個涼爽的十月天裡，姬碧和茲普看到泰弟坐在一塊石頭上，他並沒有和往常一樣的到處蹦蹦跳跳。

「泰弟，你怎麼了？」茲普問，

「我覺得怪怪的呢，」泰弟回答，「我覺得又冷又睏，彷彿自己可以睡上半年的樣子。」

October 19

One cool October day Kibby and Zip saw Tad sitting on a rock. Tad was not hopping around in his usual way.

"What's the matter, Tad?" asked Zip.

"I feel strange," said Tad. "I feel cold and sleepy. I feel as if I could sleep for half a year."

"That *is* strange," said Kibby. "I feel warm and wide awake. I feel as if I could run around all day."

"I feel like hurrying and scurrying," said Zip.

"I certainly don't feel like hurrying and scurrying," said Tad. "I wonder what is the matter with me."

「那真是怪啦，」姬碧說，「我覺得又暖又有精神，好像可以跑上一整天呢。」

茲普也說，「我倒覺得自己很急躁，好想跑來跑去呢。」

「我一點都不煩躁，更不想跑來跑去，」泰弟說，「我只想知道自己究竟是怎麼一回事。」

──────────October 20

Mother and Father Frog were sitting side by side on a rock. Tad hopped up onto the rock and sat between them.

"I think I am sick," said Tad. "I feel cold and sleepy."

"I feel cold and sleepy, too," said Mother Frog, "but I am not sick."

"I feel cold and sleepy," said Father Frog, "but I am not sick either."

青蛙爸爸和青蛙媽媽並肩坐在一塊岩石上，泰弟跳上去坐在他們的中間。

「我想我生病了，」泰弟說，「我又冷又睏呢。」

「我也是又冷又睏，」青蛙媽媽回答他，「但我好好的，沒有生病啊！」

10 / 20

"Then, if I am not sick, what am I?" cried Tad.

"You're a frog, Tad!" said Mother Frog. "Frogs always feel cold and sleepy in the fall. Soon it will be time to swim down to the bottom of Beaver Pond and go to sleep in the mud."

"I feel as if I could sleep for half a year," said Tad.

"You will," said Father Frog. "You will."

青蛙爸爸也說話了,「我一樣是又冷又睏, 也沒生病呀。」

「如果我不是生病的話, 那我是怎麼了嘛?」泰弟大叫。

「泰弟, 你是青蛙呀,」青蛙媽媽說了,「青蛙在秋天都會又冷又睏。再過一陣子, 我們就要游到「比弗池塘」底下, 睡在泥巴裡了呢。」

「我覺得自己好像可以睡上半年呢。」泰弟又說。

「會呀, 你會睡上半年的。」青蛙爸爸這麼回答著。

Hob, Nob, Bob, and Rob happened to be sitting on the top branch of Oak Tree one day when they looked up at the sky and saw a flock of geese flying by.

"It's fall," said Hob. "The geese are migrating."

"How do you migrate?" asked Nob.

10/
21

有一天，荷波、娜波、巴柏和洛柏恰好坐在「橡樹」頂的樹枝上，
觀賞著天空的景色時，他們看見一群雁鳥翩翩飛過。

「秋天了，」荷波說著，「雁鳥在遷移呢。」

"You fly from one place to another place,"
said Bob.

"Then *we* migrate all the time," said Rob.
"We fly from Oak Tree to Tall Pine, from
one maple tree to another."

"No," said Hob. "When birds migrate in the
fall, they don't just fly from tree to tree.
They fly from a cold place to a warm place
far away. It takes a long time."

「要怎麼才算是遷移呢?」娜波問,

巴柏回答:「就是從一個地方飛到另一個地方呀。」

「這樣的話,那我們一天到晚都在遷移呢,」洛柏說,「我們整天從『橡樹』飛到『大青松』,從這棵楓樹飛到另一棵楓樹。」

「不,」荷波說了,「鳥類在秋天的遷移不只是從一棵樹飛到另一棵樹而已。他們是要從一個寒冷的地方飛到一個很遙遠的溫暖地方,那得花上很多時間呢。」

Rocky Raccoon and his father were walking through the woods one day when they came to the maple tree they had tapped last March. Rocky decided to climb up into the tree.

"Be careful," said Father Raccoon.

Rocky climbed up to a big sturdy branch and sat down. He watched a bright-red maple leaf float by. He saw a crisp, brown seed pod go by on its way to the ground.

"It's fall," said Rocky. "Things are falling."

Rocky decided to see how far out on the branch he could go. When he came to the end, the branch was just a twig. The twig snapped and Rocky started to fall.

有一天浣熊洛奇和爸爸在森林散步的時候，走到了那棵他們在三月採過樹汁的楓樹前，洛奇決定要爬上樹去。

「小心喲。」浣熊爸爸說。

洛奇爬上樹，找了一根粗粗大大的樹枝坐下來。他看著一片鮮紅的楓葉在他眼前飄過，也看見一個褐色的乾豆莢和他擦身而落。

「秋天了，」洛奇說著，「東西都要掉落了呢。」

His father caught him.

"Lots of things are falling out of this tree,"
said Father Raccoon. "Leaves, seed pods,
twigs, and my favorite little raccoon."

　　洛奇要試試自己能在這根樹枝上移多遠。移呀移呀，他往外移到
盡頭時，才發現尾端只是根嫩枝；啪噠一聲嫩枝斷裂了，洛奇也跟著
墜下去。

　　浣熊爸爸一把接住了洛奇。

　　「這棵樹掉了很多東西下來唷，」浣熊爸爸說著，「有樹葉、豆莢
和樹枝，還有我心愛的小浣熊呢。」

Ten little beavers said they had nothing to do. Buck Beaver had an idea. He found a log and a board. He put the board on the log. He made a seesaw!

"Hooray!" cried ten little beavers, and they sat down—all together—on one end of the board.

Nothing happened.

"It doesn't work, Buck," said the ten little beavers.

Buck sat on the other end of the board, but nothing happened. He was bigger than any *one* of the ten little beavers, but he was not heavier than all *ten* of them.

Just then Woodsley Bear came along.

"A seesaw!" he cried. "What an excellent idea. I must try it."

十隻小河狸都說著自己沒事可做。巴克就想了個主意，他找來了一根圓木和一塊木板，把板子放在圓木上就成了一個蹺蹺板呀！

「好耶！」小河狸們大叫著，大夥全擠在板子的一端。

蹺蹺板一點動靜都沒有。

巴克坐上板子的另一端，蹺蹺板還是不動。雖然巴克比十隻小河狸中的任何一隻來得大，可是巴克還是比不上十隻小河狸加起來的重量啊。

And Woodsley Bear
sat down.

When Woodsley Bear
sat down on one end
of the seesaw, the ten
little beavers sitting
on the other end
went—UP!

大熊伍史利剛好走了過來。

「蹺蹺板!」他大叫,「這主意太棒了, 我一定得試試!」

大熊伍史利就坐了上去。

當他一坐上蹺蹺板的另一端,坐在對面的十隻小河狸就彈上去囉!

Mother Duck was talking to her ducklings.

"Children," she said. "We are about to go on a very long trip. We are going to leave Woods Hollow and fly to our winter home."

The ducklings wanted to know: "Where is our winter home?"

"It is south of here," said Mother Duck.

The ducklings wanted to know: "What is our winter home like?"

鴨媽媽正和她的小鴨們說話。

「孩子們,」她說,「我們要出遠門囉。我們要離開『哈洛小森林』, 飛到我們冬天的家。」

小鴨們都想知道:「我們冬天的家在哪裡啊?」

"It is warm and pleasant," said Mother
Duck. "There is a lake and plenty of food."
The ducklings wanted to know: "When will
we leave?"
"We can leave immediately," said Mother
Duck. "That is one of the nice things about
being a duck. We don't have to pack our
suitcases. When we fly, we travel light."

「在南方。」鴨媽媽說。

小鴨們也都想知道:「我們冬天的家是什麼樣子呢?」

「又溫暖又可愛唷,」鴨媽媽說著,「那裡有個湖, 還有充足的食
物。」

小鴨們還想知道:「我們什麼時候走呢?」

「馬上就可以走了呀,」鴨媽媽回答著,「做鴨子的好處之一就是
出門不用收拾行李。我們每回的飛行啊, 都是一趟輕便之旅呢!」

Kibby and Zip were going by Beaver Pond when they saw their friend Buck Beaver. Buck was busy making clothes.

He was not making ordinary clothes like shirts and trousers. He was making unusual clothes like witches' hats and clown outfits and cat suits.

"Why are you making those things?" asked Zip. "Who wears those kinds of clothes?"

10/25

姬碧和茲普經過「比弗池塘」的時候，看見河貍巴克正忙著做衣服。

他可不是在做襯衫啦、褲子啦，那種平常的衣服，而是在做一些很少見的衣服，像是巫婆的尖帽、小丑的全套打扮、以及小貓裝唷。

"Everybody does—on Halloween," said Buck. "The last day in October is Halloween. I am making Halloween costumes for ten little beavers."

Zip and Kibby decided that they should start thinking about their own Halloween costumes.

「你為什麼要做這些衣服?」茲普問了,「誰會穿這種衣服呢?」

「萬聖節時,每個人都會穿的呀,」巴克回答,「十月的最後一天是萬聖節,我正在替十隻小河貍做萬聖節服裝呢。」

茲普和姬碧決定開始想想他們自己的萬聖節服裝了。

Halloween was coming. Everyone in Woods Hollow began to think about Halloween costumes.

"Buffy said she would come over and show us her Halloween costume," said Kibby as she tried on her cowgirl hat. "I wonder what she will be for Halloween."

"I want to be a cowboy," said Zip. "Or a bat or a scary monster."

Just then they heard a knock at the door. Zip opened it.

There in the doorway stood someone dressed up to look like an owl.

"Oh, Buffy," cried Zip. "What a great Halloween costume! You look just like an owl. In fact, you look just like Belvedere Owl."

萬聖節就要到了,「哈洛小森林」的每個人都開始思考萬聖節要穿的服裝。

「芭菲說她要過來,讓我們瞧瞧她的萬聖節服裝哦,」姬碧邊說邊試戴她的牛仔帽,「我真想知道她在萬聖節會是什麼樣子呢。」

「我想扮成牛仔,」茲普說了,「一隻蝙蝠,或是一隻恐怖的怪獸。」

這時,他們聽到了敲門聲。茲普把門一開,門口站了一個裝扮很

"I *am* Belvedere Owl," said the guest at the door, sounding slightly offended. "I thought I would come by and ask you what you plan to be on Halloween."

像貓頭鷹的傢伙呢。

「哇！芭菲！」茲普叫了起來，「這套萬聖節服裝真棒！妳看起來就像是隻貓頭鷹。事實上，就像是貓頭鷹貝弗迪呢！」

「我就是貓頭鷹貝弗迪，」站在門口的客人說話了，語氣聽起來有點不高興唷，「我是想過來問你們萬聖節那天要扮成什麼？」

Buffy Squirrel had collected many things during the year: Rocky's empty marshmallow bags, icicles, snowballs, acorns. But the biggest thing she had collected was a pumpkin.

No one knew where the pumpkin had come from. It simply appeared one day on Buffy's doorstep.

"You should make it into a jack-o'-lantern," said Mother Squirrel.

Buffy was about to say that she did not know how to make a jack-o'-lantern when she suddenly remembered that she did.

First she cut off the top of the pumpkin and scooped out the seeds. Then she cut a face in the pumpkin—two eyes, a nose, and a big toothy smile. Finally she set a glowing candle inside.

10/
27

　　松鼠芭菲這一年裡收集了不少東西，像是洛奇的雪綿糖空袋、冰柱、雪球和堅果，但體積最大的要算她收集來的南瓜了。

　　沒人知道這南瓜來自哪裡；有一天，它就這樣出現在芭菲家的門階上了。

"This is the nicest jack-o'-lantern I have ever seen," said Buffy.

「妳可以做個南瓜燈呀。」松鼠媽媽建議著。

芭菲正要說她不知道怎麼做的時候，猛然記起自己曾經做過。

首先，她把南瓜的頂端切開來，挖出那些種子；然後在南瓜上割出一個臉的形狀——兩個眼睛、一個鼻子和一個露出牙齒的燦爛笑容。

最後，在南瓜的肚子裡放一根點燃的蠟燭。

芭菲說：「這是我見過最棒的南瓜燈了。」

Mother Chipmunk made some treats for Halloween. She dipped apples on sticks into melted caramel candy. Then she put the apples on a tray to cool.

Zip and Kibby were still trying to decide what to be on Halloween.

"I'd really like to be a cowboy," said Zip, "but maybe I will be a robot instead."

"If you two cannot decide on costumes," said Mother Chipmunk as she handed a candied apple to each of her children, "perhaps you can decide if these candied apples are good."

花栗鼠媽媽為萬聖節準備了一些可口美味的東西。她把每個蘋果插上一根棒子，往融化的焦糖裡浸一浸，再把蘋果放到托盤上冷卻。

茲普和姬碧還在研究萬聖節那天到底要扮成什麼模樣。

Zip and Kibby had no trouble deciding
about the candied apples. They were delicious!

「我真想扮成牛仔,」茲普說著,「但或許機器人也不錯呢。」

「假如你們還沒法決定你們的服裝,」花栗鼠媽媽一邊說著,一邊遞給每人一顆糖糊蘋果,「或許你們可以先決定這些糖糊蘋果好不好吃呀?」

對於這個, 茲普和姬碧可是一點問題也沒有, 因為這些糊上焦糖的蘋果太好吃囉!

萬聖節前的一兩天，每個人都在談些令人毛骨悚然的事情。

「要是「哈洛小森林」有間鬼屋就好了，」姬碧說，「那會既恐怖
又有趣呢。」

「我知道有座鬧鬼的山洞喔，」洛奇說，「就在「大岩崖」呢。」

茲普嚷著：「那就去看看呀！」

大夥都跟著洛奇來到了「大岩崖」，洛奇指出岩石間一個黑漆漆的
小洞口給他們看。

Just before Halloween everyone was talking about scary things.

"I wish we had a haunted house in Woods Hollow," said Kibby. "That would be scary—and fun!"

"I know a haunted *cave*," said Rocky. "It's at Stone Ledge."

"Let's go see it," cried Zip.

Everyone followed Rocky to Stone Ledge. He showed them a small dark opening in the rocks.

They looked in. It was dark inside.

They listened. A small rustling sound was coming from inside the cave.

What could it be?

No one wanted to go in to find out!

大夥先往洞裡看去，但裡頭也是漆黑一片；
再豎起耳朵聽，洞裡傳來了微弱的沙沙聲。
會是什麼呢？
沒有人願意進去看個究竟！

On the day before Halloween, Zip and Kibby put on their costumes and went to see Rocky Raccoon at Stone Ledge. Zip had finally decided to dress as a cowboy. Kibby was dressed as a cowgirl.

Before they reached Rocky's house, they passed the haunted cave. They stopped outside the entrance and listened. They could still hear the small rustling noise coming from inside the cave.

"Let's go in to see what's making that noise," said Kibby.

"You go first," answered Zip.

"No, *you* go first."

"Who is braver?" said Zip. "Cowboys or cowgirls?"

萬聖節的前一天，茲普和姬碧穿上他們的萬聖節服裝去拜訪在「大岩崖」的浣熊洛奇。茲普最後還是決定扮成牛仔，姬碧則是女牛仔。

在抵達洛奇家之前，他們經過了那間鬼的山洞。他們在洞口外停下來，豎起耳朵聽，洞裡傳來的沙沙聲還是很清楚喲。

「我們進去看看這聲音怎麼來的？」姬碧這麼說著。

「妳先進去，」茲普回答著。

「不，你先。」

「誰比較勇敢？」茲普說，「牛仔還是女牛仔？」

他們最後的答案就是彼此牽手，一步一步慢慢的走進去。

Kibby and Zip answered the question by holding hands and creeping slowly into the cave together.

The inside of the cave was so dark they could not see anything. But they could hear little animals moving above their heads.

Suddenly the invisible animals began flying and swooping around the cave. Then they flew right out through the cave door. Now Kibby and Zip knew what was making the noise.

Bats!

　　洞裡黑得分不清東西南北，但他們可以聽到有小動物在他們上頭動個不停。

　　突然，這些像幽靈似的動物開始在洞內亂飛亂闖，沒多久便往洞外飛出去。呼！現在茲普和姬碧知道是什麼東西發出的聲音了。

　　原來是蝙蝠呀！

October 31

On Halloween night a full yellow moon shone down on Beaver Pond. Black bats were flying and darting through the trees. Shadows moved and things creaked.

It was a dark and scary night.

Ten little beavers came out of Beaver Lodge, but they did not look like ten little beavers.

Two looked like witches with pointed hats.

萬聖節的晚上，黃澄澄的圓月映照在「比弗池塘」上，黑色蝙蝠在樹林間急速穿梭著。

到處只見陰影晃動，左右不定；怪聲怪音，吱吱亂叫著。

好一個恐怖陰森的夜晚啊！

十隻小河狸從「比弗小木屋」走出來，但他們看起來都不像是河狸呢。

兩隻看起來像是戴了尖帽的巫婆，

兩隻像鬼，兩隻像貓，

一隻像是拉了拖車的小丑，

還有三隻排成一列扮成一隻恐龍。

Two looked like ghosts and two looked like
cats.

One was a clown who was pulling a wagon.
And three went together dressed as a dragon.
Ten little beavers came out of Beaver
Lodge and headed off into the woods. And
as they went on their way that Halloween
night, they shouted:

"Trick or treat!"

　　十隻小河狸走出了「比弗小木屋」，朝著森林走去。在這萬聖節的
晚上，他們邊走邊喊著：

　　　「不請客，就搗蛋！」

【譯者註：此句為意譯，為美國萬聖節的風俗習慣。當天晚上，
　　小孩子都會裝扮成特殊的造型，成群結隊的到附近的人家敲門，
　　要求其請客吃東西；一般人習慣會準備了些糖果之類的點心，等
　　小孩子來敲門時，請些糖果打發掉。據習俗，如果不給的話，來
　　敲門的小孩子便可以對主人家惡作劇。而小孩子敲門時，說的第
　　一句話便是「Trick or treat!」】

November was a troublesome month for Belvedere Owl. The weather grew chillier and chillier. Belvedere hated the cold and did his best to ignore it. His weather predictions grew sillier and sillier.

"Start packing that picnic," Belvedere announced on the radio. "From now on we will have sunshine and blue skies."

As he said this, cold gusts of wind were blowing through the branches of Tall Pine.

"Get out your swimsuits," advised Belvedere Owl. "Today is going to be a real scorcher."

The wind began to blow with even greater force.

11 / 1

十一月對貓頭鷹貝弗迪來說是個很煩人的月份。天氣變得愈來愈冷，貝弗迪討厭冷天氣並且想盡辦法去忽略它，所以他的氣象預報也變得愈來愈可笑了。

「開始收拾東西，去野餐囉，」貝弗迪在收音機上宣布，「從現在起，我們會有大太陽和藍藍的天空呢。」

"Stay tuned for ways to beat the heat," said
Belvedere as he left to find his wool blanket.
But nothing Belvedere predicted could stop
the chilly November winds from blowing.

貝弗迪的話還沒說完，一陣冰冷的狂風吹過了「大青松」的樹枝
間。

「拿出你們的泳衣吧!」貝弗迪繼續建議，「今天會是個真正的大
熱天唷。」

風開始狂吼，一陣強過一陣。

「請繼續收聽消暑良方。」貝弗迪邊說邊去找他的羊毛毯子了，但
不管貝弗迪預報任何好天氣，都阻止不了十一月冰冷刺骨的狂風啊。

----------November 2

One windy day Kibby and Buffy decided to
fly their kite.

"Rider hasn't had any exercise for a long
time," said Kibby.

They took Rider to Snow Hill, where there
was plenty of open space to run with a kite.

Buffy held Rider in the air and started to
run. The wind caught the kite and lifted it
up. Buffy let out the string slowly. She and
Kibby watched as Rider went higher and higher.

在一個風大的日子裡，姬碧和芭菲決定去放風箏。

「『騎士』好久都沒有運動囉。」姬碧說。

她們帶著「騎士」來到了「雪丘」，因為這裡很空曠，可以盡情的
拉著風箏跑。

芭菲讓「騎士」穩穩的飄在空中後，便開始跑；風也吹著「騎士」，

As they ran this way, then that way, Rider zigzagged in the sky. Next they ran up the hill, and then they ran down the hill. Rider soared and Rider dived.

"Rider is getting a lot of exercise," said Kibby.

"So are we," added Buffy as she stopped to rest.

把它升高了。芭菲慢慢地鬆開手中的細繩，她和姬碧就看著「騎士」愈飛愈高，愈飛愈高。

她們也跟著跑呀跑，一下往這邊跑，一下往那邊跑，「騎士」因此忽左忽右的盪在空中。接著，她們跑上山坡，再跑下山坡，「騎士」也就高高的飛上去，再快速的衝下來。

「『騎士』做了很多運動呢。」姬碧說著。

「我們也一樣啊。」芭菲停下來休息時，補了這麼一句。

Woods Hollow had lost its autumn glow. The reds and yellows were gone. The leaves had turned brown and brittle and were falling off the trees. Some of the trees were already bare. Oak Tree was *almost* bare.

Mother Squirrel stepped out of her house to look for Buffy.

"Now that the leaves are almost gone," thought Mother Squirrel, "I won't have any trouble finding Buffy. She can't hide in Oak Tree anymore."

Mother Squirrel looked up. She saw the robins' old nest. She saw the sky through the branches. But she did not see Buffy.

"Buffy, where are you?" called Mother Squirrel.

11/3

「哈洛小森林」已失去了秋天的光彩，大地上看不見紅色和黃色。樹葉也披上一層棕褐色而變得乾枯易碎，掉的掉，落的落，有些樹甚至已經光禿禿的了，如「橡樹」就幾乎掉光葉子了。

松鼠媽媽走出了屋子想看看芭菲在哪裡。

「樹葉都快掉光了，」松鼠媽媽心裡想著，「要找芭菲不會有什麼困難吧，她再也無法躲在『橡樹』裡囉。」

"Here I am!" cried Buffy, popping out of a pile of dead leaves under Oak Tree. "The leaves are on the ground now, and so are my hiding places."

松鼠媽媽向上看一看,看見了知更鳥的老巢,也看見了樹枝間露出來的天空,但就是沒看見芭菲。

「芭菲,妳在哪裡呀?」松鼠媽媽叫著。

「我在這裡!」芭菲喊著,她突然從「橡樹」底下的一堆枯葉裡跳了出來,「現在樹葉都在地上,所以我躲藏的地方也就在地上囉。」

November 4

Rocky Raccoon happened to be going by the maple tree one afternoon when he saw his friends Zip and Kibby playing under the tree. They were catching leaves.

11/

4

有一天下午，浣熊洛奇碰巧經過楓樹時，看見他的朋友茲普和姬碧正在楓樹底下玩，他們正在接落葉呢。

「接到落下來的樹葉會帶來好運喔。」姬碧解釋著。

「我倒要試試看，」洛奇說，「我很想得到好運呢。」

一片鮮紅的楓葉慢慢的飄下來，洛奇看準了它。當他往前踏，接住那片葉子的時候，腳卻被一塊石頭絆倒了，他整個往後翻，跌在一

"It's good luck to catch a falling leaf," explained Kibby.

"I want to try," said Rocky. "I could use some good luck."

A bright-red maple leaf floated down. Rocky spotted it. As he stepped forward to catch the leaf, his foot tripped over a stone. He toppled backward and landed in a pile of leaves.

When he stood up, he accidentally stepped on a loose log under the leaves. The log rolled under him and Rocky tumbled off. He went flying forward and landed in the brier bush. The sharp thorns on the brier stung.

"Are you all right?" asked Zip, coming over to him.

"Sure," said Rocky, getting up. "And I didn't even drop the leaf!"

堆葉子上。

　　他要站起來的時候，不小心又踩到樹葉下一根鬆動的木頭。木頭在他腳下一滾，洛奇就跟著跌倒，向前飛了出去，落在薔薇叢裡；薔薇上的尖刺可是會刺人的呢！

　　「你還好吧?」茲普趕緊跑過來問他。

　　「當然囉，」洛奇邊說邊站了起來，「我連葉子都沒放掉呢!」

One November morning Zip poked his head out of the burrow door and saw—nothing.

"It's still dark outside," he said.

Kibby squeezed up beside Zip and looked out.

"There must be a tree growing over the doorway," she said. "It's covered by leaves."

Mother Chipmunk laughed.

"That's not a tree," she said. "It's a pile of leaves. The dead leaves have fallen off the trees and landed in our doorway."

Zip and Kibby pushed through the dead leaves until suddenly they could see the blue sky again. The morning was bright and sunny after all.

十一月的一個早上，茲普把頭伸出洞門外四處看看，但是什麼東西都沒有呀。

「外面還是黑黑的喲。」他這樣說著。

姬碧也擠在茲普的旁邊向外看出去。

「一定是門前長了棵樹，」她說，「門口都被樹葉擋住了。」

花栗鼠媽媽大笑。

「那不是樹，」她說著，「是堆落葉呢。從樹上掉下來的枯葉落在我們的門口。」

11 / 5

　　茲普和姬碧不停的撥開枯葉，直到他們能再度看到藍天的那一刻
為止。嗯，這個早上畢竟還是明亮又晴朗的喲。

Zip and Kibby sat on a log outside their burrow and stared at the piles and piles of dead leaves on the ground.

"What should we do about all these leaves?" asked Zip.

Along came Buck Beaver.

"You should rake them into a neat pile," said Buck. "That's what I would do."

Zip and Kibby were just about to find some rakes when Buffy Squirrel came along.

"You should put these leaves in a safe place," said Buffy. "Then you would have just about the biggest leaf collection anyone ever saw! And someday you might need them."

Zip and Kibby were just about to find a place to put the leaves when Rocky Raccoon came along.

茲普和姬碧坐在他們洞口外的一根大圓木上,瞪大眼睛看著地上一堆一堆的枯葉。

「我們該怎麼處理這一堆堆的葉子呀?」茲普問。

河狸巴克這時走了過來。

「你們該把葉子耙成整整齊齊的一堆呀,」巴克說,「要是我就會這樣做喲。」

茲普和姬碧正要去找些耙子來的時候,松鼠芭菲也來了。「你們該

"Here's what *I* would do with all these leaves," said Rocky, jumping into the middle of the pile. "I would play in them!"

"Raking would be helpful," said Kibby. "Collecting the leaves might be useful. But playing in them would be fun."

"Let's play!" said Zip.

把這些葉子收到一個安全的地方,」芭菲說,「這樣你們就有大家所見過最大的葉子收藏品呢! 而且, 說不定有一天你們也會需要這些葉子喔。」

　　茲普和姬碧正要去找個地方來放這些枯葉時, 浣熊洛奇也來湊熱鬧。

　　「我處理這些葉子的方法就是——,」洛奇說著就跳進這堆葉子中央,「在葉子堆裡玩呀。」

　　「把葉子耙整齊可能很有用,」姬碧說,「把葉子收藏起來也可能用的上, 但在樹葉堆裡玩會很有趣喲。」

　　「我們來玩吧!」茲普大喊著。

Woods Hollow in November was full of dead leaves. They covered the ground everywhere, and in certain places there were big piles of them.

Zip and Kibby and their friends spent one whole day just playing in them.

When they ran *through* the leaves, the leaves made a crunching sound.

11/7

「哈洛小森林」在十一月的時候到處都是枯葉，把大地的每個角落都蓋起來了，有些地方還積成一大堆呢。

茲普和姬碧還有他們的同伴們，光在這些落葉堆上就玩了一整天。

他們在葉子上面跑的時候，葉子便發出一種嘎扎，嘎扎的聲音來；

When they hid *under* the leaves, no one could see them.

When they jumped *into* the leaves, the leaves scattered in every direction.

But best of all was when they jumped off a low branch and landed *on* the leaves. The heaps of leaves were just like a soft cushion.

"Playing in the leaves was a good idea, Rocky," said Kibby.

他們躲在樹葉底下時，誰也看不見他們；

他們跳進樹葉堆時，葉子更像是仙女散花一樣，撒得到處都是。

最好玩的一招就是從一根矮樹枝上跳下來，掉在像極了軟墊子的樹葉堆上喲。

「洛奇，在這些樹葉上玩真是個好主意呢！」姬碧說。

"Tell us a story," said Kibby.

"Once upon a time," said Father Chipmunk, "there was a big golden flower named Chrysanthemum. Chrysanthemum was never in a hurry to bloom. She preferred to wait for just the right time.

「說個故事給我們聽聽。」姬碧說。

「從前，」花栗鼠爸爸說了，「有一朵金黃色的大花兒，她叫做菊花。菊花從不急著要開花，她喜歡等到適當的時間。」

「春天來了，所有東西都是新生的，還充滿了朝氣。屬於春天的

"Spring came, and everything was new and fresh. The spring flowers began to bloom. 'I will wait,' said Chrysanthemum. Summer came and everything was lush and green. The summer flowers began to grow. 'I will wait,' said Chrysanthemum. Then came the warm, golden days of autumn. 'This is my time,' said Chrysanthemum, and without any hesitation, she bloomed.

"And that is why," said Father Chipmunk, "the chrysanthemum is one of the best-known fall flowers."

The chrysanthemum is the Flower of the Month for November.

花兒都一朵朵的綻放了。菊花就說:「我要等一等。」夏天到啦,所有的東西都變得綠油油的,屬於夏季的花兒也開始一朵朵綻放了。但菊花又說:「我還要等一等。」接下來就是秋天囉,到處是一片金黃,而且暖洋洋的;菊花終於說:「嗯,這才是我的好日子。」說完就立刻把花瓣開得漂漂亮亮的。」

「也因為這樣,」花栗鼠爸爸說,「菊花就成了秋天的名花之一。」

———

菊花是代表十一月的花朵

Buffy was sitting in Oak Tree looking at the robins' nest. It had been empty for a long, long time.

Suddenly Mother Robin landed on the branch next to her.

"Did you come by to see your old nest?" asked Buffy.

"No, Buffy," said Mother Robin. "I came by to see my old friend—you!"

Mother Robin told Buffy that soon she and her family would have to leave Woods Hollow. Winter was coming.

"It is hard for us robins to find food in the winter when there is snow on the ground," said Mother Robin.

芭菲坐在「橡樹」上，看著知更鳥的舊鳥巢，它已經空了很長很長的時間呢。

突然間，知更鳥媽媽飛落在她身旁的樹枝上。

「妳是順道來看看妳的舊窩嗎?」芭菲問著。

「不，芭菲，」知更鳥媽媽說，「我是順道來看看我的老朋友——妳呀。」

知更鳥媽媽告訴芭菲，知更鳥全家很快就必須離開「哈洛小森林」，

"Why don't you collect nuts the way we squirrels do?" suggested Buffy. "Just hide them everywhere and you'll have plenty of food for winter."

"We robins are not that fond of nuts," said Mother Robin. "And it would be very hard to tell fat, juicy worms to stay where we hid them."

因為冬天就要來了。

「冬天時地上積著雪，我們知更鳥找食物會很困難的喲。」知更鳥媽媽解釋。

「你們為什麼不像松鼠一樣收集些核果呢?」芭菲建議，「只要把很多核果藏在各個角落，你們就有很多食物過冬了。」

「哎，我們知更鳥沒那麼喜歡核果，」知更鳥媽媽說，「而且，要命令那些肥美多汁的小蟲乖乖的待在我們藏牠們的地方是很困難的啊。」

November 10

Buffy decided to make a bouquet as a going-away present for Mother Robin. Of course, a spring bouquet is always full of spring flowers, but in the fall it is possible to make a different kind of bouquet—one that is full of dried plants.

Buffy collected cattails and reeds by Beaver Pond. She found other dry grasses, and seed pods on long stems. Her fall bouquet was many shades of brown and gray and white.

芭菲決定做一個花束送給知更鳥媽媽當做「遠行」的禮物。當然了，春天的花束總是放滿了春天的花朵；但是，在秋天也可以利用乾燥的植物做出不同風格的花束喔。

芭菲在「比弗池塘」旁邊撿了一些香蒲和蘆葦，也找了一些乾草

Kibby saw her. "I know what you are doing," said Kibby. "You are collecting weeds. You are starting a weed collection."

"These are not weeds," said Buffy. "Weeds are plants no one uses. I am using these plants to make a bouquet, so they can't be weeds."

和帶有長長花莖的豆莢；她的「秋之花束」是由許多深淺不同的顏色，如褐色、灰色和白色混合而成。

姬碧這時看見了她，「我知道妳在做什麼了，」姬碧說，「妳在收集雜草。哈哈，妳要開始收藏『雜草』囉。」

「這些不是雜草，」芭菲說，「雜草是沒人會拿去用的植物，我正在用這些植物來做一個花束；所以，它們就不會是雜草了。」

Kibby and Zip went to see
Buck Beaver. Buck looked
different. He was wearing
a soldier's uniform and
a soldier's hat.

"Why are you dressed
up as a soldier?"
asked Zip.

"Today is a special
day to honor soldiers,"
explained Buck.
"It is called
Veterans Day."

11/11

　　姬碧和茲普去拜訪巴克。巴克看起來很不一樣喔，他穿著軍服，
還戴了軍帽哩！

　　「你為什麼打扮得像個軍人呢？」茲普問了。

　　「今天是向軍人致敬的特別日子，」巴克解釋，「今天就是退伍軍

"What do soldiers do?"
asked Kibby.
"Soldiers protect every-
body. They keep our
country safe from enemies.
It is dangerous work,"
said Buck. "Soldiers have
to be very brave."

Buck stopped and stood
a little straighter.
"I am brave," he added.
"I keep Beaver Pond safe
for my little brothers and
sisters."

人紀念日。」

　　姬碧問：「軍人是做什麼的呢?」

　　「軍人保護著每一個人，他們維護我們國家的安全，不受敵人的
侵略，這是很危險的工作喲，」巴克說著，「軍人必須要非常勇敢呢。」

　　巴克說到這裡停了一下，站的更直一些。

　　「我很勇敢喔，」他補充說著，「我為我的弟弟妹妹們，把『比弗
池塘』保護得很安全呢。」

Tad sat on a rock next to Beaver Pond and waited for a fly to go by. He waited and waited and waited.

Along came Father Frog.

"Dad," said Tad. "How long will I have to wait before a nice, tasty fly flies by?"

"Until next spring," answered Father Frog.

"But if I sit here on this rock until next spring," said Tad, "I will probably freeze. I will also probably starve."

"You won't starve and you won't freeze," said Father Frog, "because you don't have to sit on that rock until next spring."

"I don't?" said Tad. "Then what *do* I have to do?"

"Hibernate," said Father Frog.

　　泰弟坐在「比弗池塘」旁的一塊石頭上，盼望會有蒼蠅飛過來。他等呀等著，等呀等著。

　　這個時候青蛙爸爸跳了過來。

　　「爹地，」泰弟說，「我還要等多久才會有美味可口的蒼蠅飛過來呢?」

「要等到明年春天囉，」青蛙爸爸這樣回答。

「如果我一直坐在這石頭上等到明年春天，」泰弟說，「我可能已經凍僵，也可能餓死了呀。」

「你不會凍僵，也不會餓死的，」青蛙爸爸說，「因為你不必一直坐在這裡等到明年春天啊。」

「我不必嗎？」泰弟說，「那我要做什麼呢？」

「去冬眠呀。」青蛙爸爸這樣回答。

Hob, Nob, Bob, and Rob sat on a low branch of Oak Tree and stared at the ground. They were looking for worms. The ground was covered with leaves. They waited and waited and waited, but no worms crawled out on top of the leaves.

Along came Mother Robin.

"Tell us something, Mother," said Hob. "Where are all the worms?"

11/13

荷波、娜波、巴柏和洛柏坐在「橡樹」的一根矮樹枝上,眼睛盯著地上看,找找有沒有蟲子。可是地上都蓋滿了樹葉,他們等呀,等呀,就是沒有蟲子爬到樹葉上面來。

這時候知更鳥媽媽過來了。

"The worms are asleep in the ground," said Mother Robin. "They won't come out until next spring."

"What about us?" cried Nob. "We robins have to eat. What will we do until next spring? Starve?"

"No," said Mother Robin. "We robins will fly south. We will go to a place where there is food. Flying south is what smart robins do every year."

「媽媽，這是怎麼回事，」荷波說，「蟲子都在哪裡呢？」

「蟲子都在泥土裡睡覺啊，」知更鳥媽媽說，「要等到明年春天才會爬出來呢。」

「那我們呢？」娜波叫著，「我們知更鳥總要吃呀，到明年春天以前，我們要怎麼辦呢？餓死嗎？」

「不會的，」知更鳥媽媽說著，「我們會飛到南方，到一個有食物的地方。聰明的知更鳥每年都會南飛的呀。」

Mother Raccoon helped her pupils make a map of Woods Hollow. They drew a picture of Beaver Pond at the top of the map and a picture of Stone Ledge at the bottom. They put Snow Hill in the middle.

They put all of their favorite trees on the map, too: Oak Tree, Hickory Tree, Maple Tree, Tall Pine, and Short Pine.

Zip drew a circle next to his favorite apple tree to show where he lived.

Buffy drew an X next to Oak Tree to show where she lived.

Rocky drew a wiggly square next to Stone Ledge.

"The wiggly square stands for Rocky's home," said Mother Raccoon.

11/14

浣熊媽媽幫著她的學生畫了一張「哈洛小森林」的地圖。他們在地圖的上方畫了「比弗池塘」的圖案，在地圖的下方畫上「大岩崖」的圖案，「雪丘」則畫在中間的地方。

他們也在地圖上畫了所有他們喜愛的樹木：有「橡樹」、「山胡桃樹」、「楓樹」、「大青松」和「小矮松」。

"That's not a wiggly square," said Rocky.
"That's a marshmallow."

茲普在蘋果樹的旁邊畫了個圓圈，表示這是他住的地方；
芭菲在「橡樹」的旁邊畫了個×，表示這是她住的地方；
洛奇在「大岩崖」的旁邊畫了一個歪歪斜斜的正方形。
「這歪歪斜斜的正方形代表洛奇的家。」浣熊媽媽說。
「那不是一個歪歪斜斜的正方形，」洛奇說，「那是一顆雪綿糖。」

Rocky Raccoon knew his way around Woods Hollow. He knew how to go from his house to school. He knew how to get from school to Stone Ledge.

What he did not know was what lay *beyond* Stone Ledge.

One day he decided to find out. He climbed up the rocks and down the rocks and there he was—on the other side of Stone Ledge. He was also in another part of the forest.

He decided to keep going. He was very interested in everything he saw. When he came to a creek, he turned right. When he came to a hill, he turned left. When he came to a place where the trees were thick, he kept right on going.

浣熊洛奇對「哈洛小森林」非常熟悉。他知道怎麼從自己的家到學校，也清楚要怎麼從學校走到「大岩崖」。

但是「大岩崖」的另一邊是怎樣的一個世界，他就不知道囉。

有一天洛奇決定要找出答案。他爬上岩石後，又沿著岩石爬下來，終於到「大岩崖」的另一邊啦，他還是在森林的另外一區呀。

11 / 15

But when Rocky decided to go home, he did not know which way to turn.
He was lost!

洛奇決定繼續往前走，他對看到的每樣東西都感到好奇。來到了一條小溪，他往右轉；走到了一座小山丘，他就左轉；當他來到了一個樹木密集的地方，他仍然繼續往前直走。

但是，當洛奇決定要回家的時候，卻不知道自己要轉哪一個方向呢。

他迷路啦！

Mother and Father Raccoon were very worried. It was getting dark and Rocky had not come home.

Mother Raccoon looked all along Stone Ledge. Father Raccoon went up to the top of Snow Hill and all around Beaver Pond. Together they searched all over Woods Hollow—but they did not find Rocky.

11/16

浣熊爸爸和浣熊媽媽都非常的擔心，天色愈來愈暗，洛奇還沒回家呢。

"There is someone in Woods Hollow who can help us," said Mother Raccoon. "We cannot see very well in the dark, but he can. We cannot travel on the ground very fast, but he can fly above the ground and go much faster."

"I think I know the someone you mean," said Father Raccoon. "His name is Belvedere Owl."

　　浣熊媽媽找遍了「大岩崖」，浣熊爸爸跑到「雪丘」頂上和「比弗池塘」附近所有的地方。他們還一起找遍了整個「哈洛小森林」，仍然找不到洛奇。

　　「『哈洛小森林』裡，有個人可以幫我們，」浣熊媽媽說，「我們在黑暗中看不清楚，但他可以啊；我們在地面上走得不快，但他可以高高的飛過地面，可比我們快多了。」

　　「我知道妳說的是誰了，」浣熊爸爸說，「他的名字就是——貓頭鷹貝弗迪嘛。」

November 17

Belvedere Owl was flying through the
darkness on a very important mission—to
find Rocky Raccoon.

貓頭鷹貝弗迪在黑暗中飛翔著，這一次他可是有很重要的任務喔
——去找浣熊洛奇呀。

他飛過了「比弗池塘」，找過了「大青松」，飛到了「大岩崖」的
另一邊。

飛行的時候，他的眼睛都一直朝地面上看哨，

「還好我們貓頭鷹能夠在黑暗中看東西，」貝弗迪心裡這樣想著。

突然間，他看見有東西在動，看起來很像熟悉的胖浣熊呢！貝弗

He flew past Beaver Pond. He flew past
Tall Pine. He flew beyond Stone Ledge.

As he flew he kept his eyes turned toward
the ground.

"It's lucky we owls can see in the dark,"
thought Belvedere.

Suddenly he saw something moving. It
looked like a familiar fat raccoon. Belvedere
swooped down. Sure enough, there was
Rocky, walking in the dark and looking scared.

He was so glad to see Belvedere Owl!

Belvedere showed him the way home.

Do you think Mother and Father Raccoon
were glad to see Rocky?

迪趕緊衝下來。沒錯，洛奇就在那兒！他正走在黑暗中，一副已經嚇
得半死的樣子。

洛奇看到貓頭鷹貝弗迪好高興喲！

貝弗迪引導著洛奇走回家。

你想，浣熊爸爸和浣熊媽媽看到洛奇會高興嗎？

One morning the weather was so cold and damp that Kibby and Zip decided to stay indoors. Kibby was painting pictures while Zip worked on some science experiments.

"See my red sailboat on a blue lake," said Kibby, holding up the picture she had painted.

Zip had filled a container with water. He wanted to see what things would float and what things would sink. He put some pebbles on the water. The pebbles sank. He put some empty nutshells on the water. *They* floated.

Kibby decided to paint one of the nutshells red. She cut out a white paper sail and attached it to a tiny stick. She glued the stick to the inside of the nutshell. Then she put it back on the water.

有一天早上，天氣實在是又冷又濕，姬碧和茲普決定待在室內。姬碧畫著圖，茲普則做一些科學實驗。

姬碧拿起她畫好的圖畫說：「你看，我的紅色帆船在藍色的湖上呢。」

茲普在一個桶裡裝滿了水，他想看看哪些東西會浮起來，哪些會沈下去。他放了小石子在水中，小石子沈了下去；他再放一些空的核

"Now I have a real red sailboat on a little lake," she said, pointing to the nutshell sailboat.

果殼在水中，核果殼全部都浮起來。

　　姬碧決定把其中的一個核果殼塗成紅色。她剪了一個白色的紙帆，把這白紙做的帆用膠水黏在一根小小的棒子上，再把這枝小棒子黏在核果殼的裡面。弄好後，姬碧把核果殼放回水裡。

　　她指著這艘核果殼做的帆船說：「現在我有一艘真正的紅帆船在小湖上了哦。」

Zip and Kibby gave a going-away party for Tad.

Zip made fruit salad, and Kibby made a nut and berry snack.

Rocky Raccoon came early and brought a marshmallow pie.

Buffy Squirrel came on time and brought four trays of sandwiches.

11 / 19

茲普和姬碧為泰弟舉辦了一個歡送會。

茲普做了水果沙拉，姬碧做了堅果加漿果點心；

浣熊洛奇來的早，還帶了一盤雪綿糖派；

"I think we will have too much food," said Kibby.

But then Buck Beaver came late, bringing all ten of his brothers and sisters.

"We don't have too much food now," said Kibby. "What we need is a few more places to sit."

松鼠芭菲準時到，也帶了四盤三明治。

姬碧說：「我們有太多食物了！」

但遲到的巴克帶著十個弟弟妹妹出現了，

「現在我們的食物不會太多囉，」姬碧說著，「我們現在需要的是再多幾個位子坐呢。」

Tad was going away for the winter. He was going to hibernate at the bottom of Beaver Pond.

"Have fun!" cried Buffy Squirrel.

"Frogs don't have fun while they hibernate," said Tad.

"Eat well!" cried Rocky Raccoon.

"Frogs don't eat at all while they hibernate," said Tad.

"Send us a postcard now and then!" called Buck Beaver.

"Frogs don't do much writing while they hibernate," said Tad.

"Then, what in the world do frogs do when they hibernate?" asked Kibby and Zip.

"They sleep," said Tad. "Good-bye. See you next spring!"

11 / 20

泰弟就要離開去過冬了,他要在「比弗池塘」的池底冬眠。

「好好的玩!」松鼠芭菲大聲的說。

「青蛙冬眠的時候沒什麼好玩的。」泰弟回答。

「吃好一點哦!」浣熊洛奇大聲的說。

「青蛙冬眠時，都不吃東西的呀。」泰弟回答。

「偶爾寄張明信片給我們喲！」河狸巴克喊著。

「青蛙冬眠時，也不寫東西的呀。」泰弟這樣回答。

「那麼青蛙冬眠時，到底在做什麼呢?」姬碧和茲普問。

「就是睡覺呀，」泰弟說著，「再見囉，明年春天見！」

November 21

Mother and Father Robin were getting ready to leave Woods Hollow. Buffy came by to say good-bye.

"When will you be back?" asked Buffy.

"As soon as the weather turns warmer," said Father Robin.

"Are you sure you'll be back?" asked Buffy.

11 / 21

知更鳥爸爸和媽媽已經準備好要離開「哈洛小森林」了，芭菲來向他們說再見。

「你們什麼時候會回來呢?」芭菲問，

知更鳥爸爸說:「天氣一變暖，我們就回來了。」

"Of course," said Mother Robin. "This is where we robins like to raise our families. This is our home. We love the trees and the bushes. We love the pond and the rocks and the soft earth."

"And," added Father Robin, "we especially love the earth*worms!*"

As Mother and Father Robin flew off to their winter place, Buffy called out, "See you in the spring!"

「你們確定會回來嗎?」芭菲又問,

「當然啦,」知更鳥媽媽說,「我們喜歡在這裡養兒育女,這是我們的家呢。我們喜歡這裡的樹木和灌木,也喜歡這裡的池塘、岩石和鬆軟軟的泥土。」

「而且,」知更鳥爸爸加上一句,「我們特別喜歡這裡的蚯蚓喲!」

當知更鳥爸爸和媽媽飛往他們過冬的地方時,芭菲喊著:「我們春天見囉!」

November 22

Thanksgiving came at the end of November. It was a very special time in Woods Hollow— a time to feel thankful, a time for feasting.

Thanksgiving was also a time to be together. Being together meant eating together, and eating together meant finding an extra-long table.

感恩節是在十一月底。

在「哈洛小森林」，這是一個很特別的時刻，它不僅是一個感恩的時刻，也是一個享受美食的時刻。

感恩節更是大夥聚在一起的好時刻。

聚在一起的意思就是在一起吃吃喝喝，要在一起吃吃喝喝，就得找一張特別長的桌子。

Buck Beaver made one out of some leftover
logs. He made a long table and two long
benches, one for each side of the table.

Buck hauled the table and the benches all
the way to the apple tree near the Chipmunk
family's house. The Thanksgiving feast was
to be held there.

"We are celebrating Thanksgiving in our
own back yard," said Zip as he came out of
his house.

河狸巴克就用剩下的木頭，做了一張這樣的桌子。他一共做了一
張長桌子和兩張長凳，桌子的每一邊各有一張長凳呢。

巴克把長桌子和長凳一直拖到花栗鼠家附近的蘋果樹旁，因為感
恩節大餐將在那裡舉行喲。

「我們是在自己的後院慶祝感恩節呢。」茲普從屋裡走出來時，高
興的說著。

Everyone brought something to eat for the Thanksgiving feast.

The Chipmunk family brought berries—berry jam, berry pie, and berry pudding. The Raccoon family brought fish and corn and mushrooms. Mother Squirrel and Buffy Squirrel came loaded down with so many nuts that no one could see who was carrying them.

11 / 23

感恩節的宴會上，每個人都會帶些東西來。

花栗鼠一家帶了各式各樣的漿果，像是果醬、漿果派和漿果布丁；浣熊一家帶來了鮮魚和玉米；松鼠媽媽和松鼠芭菲也到了，她們的肩膀上堆了太多的核果，所以沒有人看清楚到底是誰扛著這些核果。

Belvedere Owl flew in with a basket of grapes. Grandpa Ground Hog arrived with corn. There were apples and acorns, seeds and cider. Buck Beaver and his brothers and sisters brought woodchip soup.

"But Buck," said Zip. "You already brought something—the table!"

貓頭鷹貝弗迪提了一籃葡萄，飛了過來；

土撥鼠老爹帶了玉米來。

這個感恩節大餐還有蘋果、堅果、種子和蘋果汁等，一大堆的東西喲。

河狸巴克和他的弟弟妹妹帶了木屑湯過來，

「喂，巴克，」茲普說：「你早已經帶了東西呀——這桌子嘛！」

The Thanksgiving table was covered with good things to eat. Buffy set a few pine cones and fall leaves in the middle of the table to decorate it.

Zip and Kibby set a plate at each place. Rocky Raccoon made name cards to put next to each plate.

為感恩節準備的桌子上擺滿了好吃的東西，芭菲還在桌子中間放了一些松果和落葉當做裝飾。

茲普和姬碧在每個位置前放一個盤子，浣熊洛奇則做了一些名牌放在每個盤子的旁邊。

Buck Beaver showed up with his arms full of things—bark, twigs, leaves, and roots.

"Thanks, Buck," said Buffy. "These things will make great decorations."

"Decorations?" cried Buck. "These are not for decorations. These things are food. Beavers like to eat bark and twigs and leaves and roots."

"I'm thankful I'm a squirrel," said Buffy. "I am not really fond of eating wood."

河狸巴克來了，雙手抱滿東西，有樹皮、樹枝、樹葉，還有樹根。

「巴克，謝謝啦，」芭菲說，「這些東西會是很棒的裝飾品喲！」

「裝飾品?」巴克大叫，「這些東西可不是用來做裝飾的，它們是食物呢。河狸都愛吃樹皮、樹葉和樹根的。」

「哇！謝天謝地，我是一隻松鼠，」芭菲說著，「我實在不怎麼喜歡吃樹木呢。」

On Thanksgiving Day everyone sat down at the long table to feast and to celebrate. Just as they were about to begin, they heard a familiar sound. The *thump, thump, thump* of big bear feet coming through the woods.

"It's Woodsley!" cried Kibby.

And it was. Woodsley Bear had come to join them.

"Did you finish writing the book about Woods Hollow?" asked Buffy.

"Not yet," said Woodsley. "I still have to tell about how the inhabitants of Woods Hollow celebrated Thanksgiving."

"We celebrated it with Woodsley Bear," said Buffy. "You can write about that."

感恩節當天，每個人都坐在長桌前享受美食和慶祝佳節。正當他們要開始的時候，聽見了一個很熟悉的聲音。砰，砰，砰，一隻大熊的腳步聲自森林裡傳來。

「嘿，是伍史利!」姬碧叫著。

果然是他! 大熊伍史利也來參加宴會。

「你寫完了那本關於『哈洛小森林』的書嗎?」芭菲問，

　　「還沒呢，」伍史利回答，「我還要寫一些『哈洛小森林』的居民是如何慶祝感恩節的事呢。」

　　「我們是和你——大熊伍史利一起慶祝的啊，」芭菲說，「你可以把這個寫下來呀。」

November 26

"I'm thankful," said Woodsley Bear, "to have so many wonderful friends in Woods Hollow."

「我很感謝在『哈洛小森林』有那麼多的好朋友，」大熊伍史利向大家說著。

感恩節是表達謝意的時候，也是每個人在享受美食之後要做的一件事呢。

花栗鼠媽媽看著她的兩個孩子說：「我很感謝我的兒子和女兒。」

「我們也很感謝媽媽和爸爸，」姬碧看著爸爸媽媽這樣回答。

「嗯……」芭菲說，「我要感謝那些核果。」

Thanksgiving was a time to give thanks—
and everyone, having eaten and eaten, was
doing just that.

"I'm thankful for sons and daughters," said
Mother Chipmunk, looking at her two children.

"And we're thankful for mothers and
fathers," said Kibby, looking at her parents.

"Well," said Buffy. "I'm thankful for nuts."

Buck stood up. "I'm thankful for trees. We
beavers depend upon trees for food, for
shelter, for everything we need. We couldn't
get along without trees."

"I think we should all be thankful that
Woods Hollow is such a nice, safe, cozy place
to live," said Father Raccoon.

巴克站起來說:「我很謝謝那些樹木。我們河狸所需要的每一樣東
西,如食物啦、房子啦,都得依靠樹木。沒有樹木,我們就沒辦法生
活。」

「我想我們都應該感謝『哈洛小森林』,它是這麼的漂亮、安全和
舒服,真是居住的好地方呢!」浣熊爸爸說了這一句話。

The Thanksgiving feast was not quite over. It was time for dessert.

"What's for dessert?" asked Rocky Raccoon.

"Pie!" answered Father Chipmunk. "We have apple pie, berry pie, pumpkin pie, and acorn pie."

"What about marshmallow pie?" said Rocky.

"We don't have any marshmallow pie," said Father Chipmunk.

"Yes, we do," said Rocky. "I brought it. I carried a marshmallow pie all the way from my house. It was in a big red pie plate."

Father Chipmunk held up a big red pie plate. The pie plate was empty.

"Ooops!" said Rocky. "I forgot. I *brought* a marshmallow pie, but I also *ate* a marsh-mallow pie."

感恩節大餐還沒有完全結束，吃甜點的時間到囉。

「有什麼甜點呀?」浣熊洛奇問，

「派呀!」花栗鼠爸爸回答，「有蘋果派、漿果派、南瓜派和堅果派。」

「那雪綿糖派呢?」洛奇又問，

　　「我們沒有雪綿糖派耶。」花栗鼠爸爸說。

　　「我們有呀，」洛奇說，「我帶來了呀。我從家裡一路帶著雪綿糖派來的，它是放在一個紅色的大盤子上。」

　　花栗鼠爸爸拿起一個紅色的大盤子，但盤子是空的。

　　「哎呀，我忘了，」洛奇說，「我是帶了雪綿糖派，但我也吃掉了雪綿糖派。」

After the Thanksgiving feast, everybody helped to clean up. They put away leftover food. They washed and dried the dishes and tucked them into cupboards.

Buck was all ready to take the table and benches back to Beaver Pond when he noticed something still on the table.

感恩節大餐後，每個人都幫忙清理。他們把剩下來的食物收好，盤子洗乾淨放回碗櫥裡。

巴克正準備把桌子和長凳搬回「比弗池塘」的時候，注意到還有東西在桌子上。

Grandpa Ground Hog!

While they had been working, Grandpa Ground Hog—full of nuts and berries and apple pie—had gone to sleep. But it wasn't a little after-dinner nap he was taking. Grandpa Ground Hog had begun his long winter's sleep.

He was hibernating on the log table.

z-z-z-z

土撥鼠老爹！

當大家在忙的時候，吃了一肚子的核果、漿果和蘋果派的土撥鼠老爹已經呼呼大睡了。這可不是晚餐後的小睡而已，土撥鼠老爹已經開始了他長長的冬季睡眠呢。

他就在那長桌上冬眠囉！

Everyone was trying to wake up Grandpa Ground Hog.

"Wake up, Grandpa Ground Hog," whispered Kibby.

But Grandpa Ground Hog did not stir.

"It's time to go home," said Zip in a louder voice.

But Grandpa Ground Hog did not budge.

"ATTENTION, ALL GROUND HOGS!" shouted Buck Beaver.

Ever so slowly Grandpa Ground Hog woke up. He blinked his eyes and sniffed the air. He began to look for his shadow. He thought February had already arrived.

"It's going to be an early spring," he told everyone.

每個人都試著叫醒土撥鼠老爹。

「起來呀，土撥鼠老爹!」姬碧輕輕喊著，

但土撥鼠老爹動也不動。

「該回家囉!」茲普把聲音提高了一點，

但土撥鼠老爹還是動都不動。

「全體土撥鼠，注意!」巴克大吼了，

"But Grandpa Ground Hog," said Zip. "We haven't had winter yet. You've only been asleep for an hour! You have to go home to your burrow. Then you can go to sleep for the winter."

Grandpa Ground Hog, recognizing good advice when he heard it, did exactly that.

慢慢地，慢慢地，土撥鼠老爹醒來了。他眨眨眼睛，嗅了嗅空氣，開始尋找他的影子，他以為二月已經來了呢。

「嗯，今年的春天來得真早唷，」他告訴大家。

「但是，土撥鼠老爹，」茲普說話了，「冬天還沒來呢，你只是睡了一個小時而已！你得回家去，回到你的地洞裡，然後你就可以睡上一整個冬天了。」

土撥鼠老爹聽了覺得這是個好主意，也就照做了。

On the last day of November everyone in Woods Hollow, except those who were already asleep, raked leaves.

Zip and Kibby raked the leaves from the apple tree next to their house.

Buffy raked leaves from Oak Tree.

Rocky raked leaves that had drifted up against Stone Ledge.

Buck and his brothers and sisters brought pile after pile of dead leaves to Snow Hill. Zip and Kibby brought their leaves. Buffy brought hers. Rocky added even more leaves to the pile.

The pile of leaves on Snow Hill grew and grew.

在十一月的最後一天，除了那些已經睡著的人以外，「哈洛小森林」的每個人都在用耙子聚集落葉。

茲普和姬碧在耙他們家旁邊的蘋果樹。

芭菲在耙「橡樹」落下的枯葉。

洛奇在耙那些堆在「大岩崖」的落葉。

巴克和他的弟弟妹妹們把一堆一堆的樹葉搬到「雪丘」上，茲普

That night Father Raccoon set fire to the leaves. It was a beautiful bonfire. Everyone stood and watched it glow—there on the top of Snow Hill.

和姬碧也把耙好的樹葉搬上去，芭菲也搬來她的樹葉，洛奇則在這堆落葉上加了更多的落葉。

「雪丘」上的落葉愈堆愈大，愈堆愈大。

那天晚上，浣熊爸爸點火燒那堆落葉，那可是很美的營火喲。於是大家都站起來，在「雪丘」的頂上看著這營火燃燒。

December 1

It was the first day of December. Zip and Kibby were studying the calendar.

"Christmas is coming," said Kibby. "The twenty-fifth day of this month is my favorite day of the year."

"Mine, too," said Zip. "And it is only twenty-four more days away."

"Think of all the things we can do," said Kibby. "We can make Christmas presents and write Christmas cards. We can decorate the Christmas tree. We can bake Christmas cookies."

"Let's keep track of all the things we make," said Zip. "Let's count the presents and the cards and the cookies, too."

十二月的第一天,兹普和姬碧正仔細看著日曆。

「聖誕節快到了唷,」姬碧說,「這個月的第二十五天是我一年之中最喜歡的日子了。」

「我也是,」兹普說,「離現在只剩二十四天了。」

「想想,我們可以做好多事呢。」姬碧說,「我們可以做些聖誕禮物,寫聖誕卡,也可以好好的裝飾聖誕樹,更可以烤些聖誕節餅乾。」

「讓我們把要做的一切都寫清楚,」兹普說,「我們要數清楚有多少禮物,多少張卡片和多少餅乾唷。」

"I have an idea," said Kibby. "Let's count the days until Christmas."

「我還有個主意呢，」姬碧說，「我們來每天數日子直到聖誕節來臨。」

Zip and Kibby went to see their friend Buck Beaver. They found him cutting down a tree.

"Hmmm," said Kibby. "That's a nice tree. I wonder what you will use it for. Let me guess. Are you planning to make some repairs on Beaver Dam? Is it going to hold up the roof in Beaver Lodge?"

"I have a better idea," said Zip. "Maybe you are going to make a big pot of woodchip soup—so big you have to start with a whole tree."

茲普和姬碧去看河狸巴克的時候，發現他正在鋸一棵樹。

「嗯，」姬碧說，「這棵樹好漂亮！奇怪了，你要用來做什麼呢？我來猜猜看，你打算拿去修補『比弗水壩』？還是拿去支撐『比弗小木屋』的屋頂？」

「我有個更好的主意，」茲普說，「說不定你想要做一大鍋的木屑湯；因為要好大一鍋，所以你得先準備一整棵樹。」

"No, no, no," said Buck. "This tree will never be anything but a tree, because it's a very special tree. Can't you tell by its shape what kind of a tree it is?"

Zip and Kibby looked carefully at the tree. It was a fir tree with beautiful full branches from top to bottom.

"It's a Christmas tree!" they cried.

「都不是,」巴克說,「這棵樹永遠會是一棵樹,不會變成別的東西啦, 因為它是一棵很特別的樹。難道你們沒法從它的形狀看出它是哪一種樹嗎?」

茲普和姬碧仔細的注視這棵樹。它是一棵樅樹,整棵樹都長了很美麗、很茂盛的樹枝。

「它是棵聖誕樹!」他們叫著。

-------------------------- December 3

Not much was happening at Hickory Hive.
Gone were the flower dances of spring and
summer. Now that the weather outside was
chilly, B.G. and the other bees were interested
in only one thing—staying warm.

They crowded together inside the hive and
buzzed rapidly. The rapid buzzing made a
kind of hum which filled the hive. It also

「山胡桃蜂房」並沒發生什麼大不了的事情，春夏兩季花兒飄舞
的景色已不再。現在，外面的氣溫好冷唷，比姬和其他的蜜蜂只對保
暖這一件事感興趣。

他們在蜂房內擠成一堆，快速的拍動著雙翅，這種嗡嗡聲充滿了
蜂房的每一個角落，也因此形成一種熱氣來唷。藉著大家日夜不停的
一起拍動，蜜蜂便可以保暖了。

made a kind of heat. By buzzing together, day and night, the bees stayed warm.

It took a lot of energy to do so much buzzing. Where did B.G. and the other bees get all their energy?

They had worked hard in the spring and summer, and now the honeycomb was well stocked with honey. The bees ate up their stores of honey in the winter.

The honey gave them energy.

　　但這樣不停的搧動翅膀要花上很多的體力，比姬和其他的蜜蜂哪來的體力呢？

　　原來啊，他們在春天和夏天都辛勤地工作，所以現在蜂巢都儲滿了蜂蜜；冬天的時候，蜜蜂就會吃光蜂蜜。

　　蜂蜜就帶給他們體力了呀。

December 4

The fir tree that Buck Beaver had brought to Beaver Lodge stood in the middle of the room. Buck had fastened tiny lights to many of its branches. Now ten little beavers were making decorations to put on its boughs.

河狸巴克把搬回「比弗小木屋」的樅樹直立在房子的中央。他在比較細的樹枝上綁了許多的小燈泡，十隻小河狸現在正做著各種裝飾品要擺在比較粗的樹枝上呢。

Two were making paper chains. Two were
placing candy canes on the Christmas tree.
Two were hanging silver balls. Two were
cutting paperdolls.

One was cutting snowflakes from white paper.
One was making gold stars out of shiny paper.

"I like all the things that go on the
Christmas tree," said one of the little beavers.

"I like all the things that go *under* the
Christmas tree," said another little beaver.

兩隻小河貍正做著一長串的紙環，兩隻小河貍把拐杖糖放在聖誕
樹上，另外兩隻小河貍則負責掛上銀色的球，還有兩隻小河貍正剪著
紙娃娃。

一隻小河貍用白紙剪下一片片的雪花。

最後一隻小河貍則用發亮的紙做出一顆顆金光閃閃的星星唷。

「我喜歡放在聖誕樹上的所有東西。」其中一隻小河貍說。

「我喜歡放在樹下的所有東西。」另外一隻小河貍說。

Kibby and Zip were making Christmas cards. Mother Chipmunk showed them how to draw Christmas trees.

They drew Christmas trees on green paper. They drew Christmas balls on red paper. After they drew the trees and the balls, they cut them out.

Next they made cards. They folded big pieces of white paper to make big cards. They folded little pieces of white paper to make little cards.

Then they glued the trees to the cards. Next they glued the balls to the trees. Kibby drew presents under one tree. Zip drew a Santa next to another. They made all the cards look a little different from one another.

Inside each card they wrote—**MERRY CHRISTMAS!**

姬碧和兹普正在動手做聖誕卡片，花栗鼠媽媽則指導他們如何畫聖誕樹。

他們在綠色的紙上畫聖誕樹，在紅色的紙上畫聖誕球。畫好之後，便把它們一一剪下來。

接下來，便是做卡片囉。他們把大張的白紙摺成大張的卡片，小張的白紙摺成小張的卡片。

　　然後，把剪下來的樹分別用膠水黏在各張卡片上，再把聖誕球用
膠水黏在卡片的樹上。姬碧在一棵樹下畫了一些禮物，茲普在另一棵
樹旁畫上聖誕老公公。

　　他們讓所有的卡片看起來都有一點點不同。

　　每張卡片裡面，他們都寫著聖誕快樂。

Father Raccoon was making gingerbread cookies for Christmas. He had cut the cookie dough into many different shapes.

"May I try a gingerbread Santa?" asked Rocky when the cookies came out of the oven. "I haven't tasted one yet."

"The gingerbread Santa tastes the same as the gingerbread star and the gingerbread bell and the gingerbread Christmas tree," said Father Raccoon.

浣熊爸爸在準備聖誕節要吃的薑餅，他把生麵糰切成各種不同的形狀。

「我可以嚐一塊『聖誕老人』薑餅嗎？」當餅乾出爐時，洛奇問著，「我還沒嚐過呢。」

「『聖誕老人』薑餅的味道吃起來和星星薑餅，鈴鐺薑餅，聖誕樹薑餅都一模一樣呀。」浣熊爸爸說。

"Are you sure?" asked Rocky.

Father Raccoon gave Rocky a gingerbread Santa. Rocky tasted it.

"You're right," said Rocky. "The gingerbread Santa does taste the same. Now I know for sure that all gingerbread cookies have the same flavor."

Father Raccoon laughed and took another batch of the cookies out of the oven.

"Oh boy! Gingerbread snowmen!" cried Rocky. "May I try a gingerbread snowman, Father? I haven't tasted one yet."

「你確定嗎?」洛奇問,

浣熊爸爸就拿給洛奇一塊「聖誕老人」薑餅,洛奇嚐了幾口。

「沒錯呢,」洛奇說,「『聖誕老人』薑餅的味道真的一模一樣! 我現在肯定所有薑餅的味道都是一樣的。」

浣熊爸爸笑了起來,然後取出另外一爐的餅乾。

「哇,雪人薑餅!」洛奇叫了起來,「爸爸,我可以嚐一塊雪人薑 餅嗎? 我還沒嚐過呢。」

December 7

Zip and Kibby met their friend Rocky in the woods. While they were talking, Kibby noticed something different about Rocky.

"Rocky, you are taller than you used to be," she said.

"That's because I have been growing," said Rocky.

"You are also fatter than you used to be," said Zip.

茲普和姬碧在森林裡遇見了他們的朋友洛奇，他們便聊了起來，姬碧注意到洛奇有些不一樣呢。

她說：「洛奇，你比以前高了呢。」

「那是因為我一直在長大啊。」洛奇說。

茲普說：「你也比以前胖了。」

"That's because I have been eating so
much," said Rocky. "We raccoons have to
store up food for the winter. Then when we
take long naps, we won't be hungry. We can
just rest and dream about—marshmallows!"

"Rocky may be taller and fatter," said Zip.
"But there is one thing about Rocky that has
not changed. He still thinks about
marshmallows every day of the year."

「那是因為我都吃很多啊,」洛奇說,「我們浣熊必須要儲存食物
來過冬,所以冬天睡大覺的時候,肚子就不會餓囉。我們可以好好的
休息,而且還能夢見雪綿糖呢。」

「洛奇或許長高、長胖了,」茲普說,「但洛奇有一點不會變的,
就是他每天都還是想著雪綿糖呢。」

Every job has its slow times and its busy times. Mother Squirrel's job—collecting and delivering the mail—kept her busiest at Christmas.

Not only were Zip and Kibby sending Christmas cards to all of their cousins in different forests far away, but all of their cousins were sending Christmas cards to Zip and Kibby.

There were big cards and little cards, cards in white envelopes and cards in green envelopes. There were cards addressed to Rocky Raccoon and cards addressed to Buffy Squirrel. And that was not all.

There were packages, too.

每一份工作都會有它空閒的時候以及忙碌的時候。對松鼠媽媽那份收信、送信的工作來說，最忙的時刻就是聖誕節了。

不只是茲普和姬碧寄聖誕卡給遠在不同森林的表兄妹，他們表兄妹也會寄聖誕卡給茲普和姬碧呢。

卡片有大有小；有用白信封裝的，也有用綠信封裝的；有寄給浣熊洛奇的，也有寄給松鼠芭菲的；這還不是全部喲。

Aunt and Uncle Raccoon sent Rocky Raccoon a package. When Mother Squirrel delivered it, she gave it a shake.

"Hmmmm," she said, "I bet I know what is inside *this* package. It is something soft and white and sweet."

Can you guess what it was?

還有些包裹呢!

浣熊叔叔和姑姑寄給浣熊洛奇一個包裹,當松鼠媽媽在送這個包裹的時候,把它搖了一搖。

「嗯,」她說,「我敢打賭,我知道這包裏裡面是什麼東西! 它是一種軟軟的,白白甜甜的東西呢。」

你猜得出來是什麼嗎?

December 9

Buffy Squirrel went down to get the mail. She found a big package from Grandfather Squirrel, who lived in an old oak tree beyond Stone Ledge. There were Christmas cards from her friends and relatives. And there was a postcard from a place far away.

On the front of the postcard she saw a picture of a grassy meadow. In the meadow there were flowers, trees, and a small brook.

On the back of the postcard there was a message—a letter to Buffy. It said:

松鼠芭菲走下來拿她的信件。她發現有一個松鼠爺爺寄來的包裹，松鼠爺爺就住在「大岩崖」另一邊的一棵老橡樹裡。也有從朋友親戚那裡寄來的聖誕卡，還有一張從很遠的地方寄來的明信片。

在明信片的正面，她看到了一幅圖畫：有著一片綠油油的草地，草地裡有花，有樹以及一條小溪流。

在明信片的背面，有一段話是寫給芭菲的，它是這樣寫的：

DEAR BUFFY,
GREETINGS FROM GRASSY MEADOW!
WE ARE HAVING A GREAT TIME HERE.
IT IS WARM AND THERE IS PLENTY TO EAT.
BUT WE MISS OUR FRIENDS IN WOODS
HOLLOW. SEE YOU NEXT SPRING!
HOB, NOB, BOB, AND ROB

PAR AVION

Buffy Squirrel
Oak Tree
Woods Hollow

Squirrels
OAK
TREE

親愛的芭菲：

這是來自「綠草牧場」的祝福！我們在此地過得很愉快。這裡很
暖和，也有很多東西吃。但是我們很想念我們在「哈洛小森林」的朋
友。明年春天見囉！

荷波、娜波、巴柏和洛柏敬上

Mother Raccoon was teaching the pupils at Woods Hollow School how to read.

She wrote the word **TREE** on the board.

"Who can read this word?" said Mother Raccoon.

Ten little beavers looked at the word **TREE**, but no one was able to read it.

Mother Raccoon wrote the word **LOG** on the board.

"Who can read this word?" said Mother Raccoon.

Ten little beavers looked at the word **LOG**, but no one offered to read it.

Then Mother Raccoon wrote the words **MERRY CHRISTMAS** on the board. She wanted to wish everyone a happy holiday.

"We can read *that*!" cried ten little beavers. **"MER—RY CHRIST—MAS!"**

浣熊媽媽在教「哈洛小森林學校」的學生如何閱讀。

她在黑板上寫了一個「TREE」（樹木）這個字。

浣熊媽媽問：「誰會唸這個字？」

十隻小河狸睜大了眼睛看著「TREE」這個字，但沒有一個會唸。

浣熊媽媽又在黑板上寫「LOG」（圓木）這個字，但也沒有哪一個表示會唸。

12/
10

　　然後浣熊媽媽又在黑板上寫「MERRY　CHRISTMAS」（聖誕快
樂）這幾個字。她希望祝福每一個人都有個快樂的假期。

　　「我們會唸那個！」十隻小河狸高聲大喊，「MER—RY—CHRIST
—MAS!（聖誕快樂）」

Every Christmas, Mother and Father Chipmunk always brought home the Christmas presents and hid them. And every Christmas, Zip and Kibby tried very hard to find them.

One day Zip and Kibby decided to try looking in their own closet. Because it was always in such a mess, their parents might just think it would be a good hiding place.

The first thing Zip and Kibby saw when they opened the closet door was a box marked NOISEMAKERS.

"That box makes me think of the end of the year," said Kibby. "And the end of the year reminds me that it's time to think about New Year's resolutions."

每年聖誕節，花栗鼠媽媽和爸爸都帶了很多禮物回家並把它們藏起來。茲普和姬碧在每年的聖誕節，也很努力的試著把這些禮物找出來。

有一天，茲普和姬碧決定去翻翻他們的櫃子，因為那裡老是一團亂，說不定他們的爸爸媽媽認為這會是藏東西的好地方哩。

打開櫃門，茲普和姬碧看見的第一件東西是上頭寫了「吹打用具」的盒子。

12/11

"Last year we said we were going to clean this closet," answered Zip. "And we finally did. Maybe next year we should resolve to keep it clean all year long."

「那個盒子使我想起一年就要結束了，」姬碧說，「而想到一年就要結束提醒了我，該是想想『新年新希望』的時候囉。」

「去年我們說過要清理這個櫃子的，」茲普回答，「雖然我們最後還是把它清理好了，但也許明年我們該下決心把櫃子一整年都保持乾淨。」

Kibby and Zip were still searching for their Christmas presents.

Zip lifted up a pile of clothes. Under the clothes he found a red sled.

姬碧和兹普還在找他們的聖誕禮物。

兹普拿起一堆衣服，發現了放在衣服堆下面的紅雪橇。

「我們今天不能去玩雪橇呀，」兹普說，「『雪丘』上沒有雪。」

姬碧又拉又扯的把壓在玩具箱下面的東西拉了出來，原來是一艘橡皮艇。

「我們也不能把橡皮艇帶去『比弗池塘』呀，」姬碧說，「要等到

"We can't go sledding today," said Zip. "There's no snow on Snow Hill."

Kibby tugged and pulled on something that was stuck under a box of toys. Out came a rubber raft.

"We can't take our raft to Beaver Pond," said Kibby. "We'll have to wait until next summer when it's warmer."

Zip took a suitcase out of the closet and opened it. Inside he found their cowboy and cowgirl costumes.

"We can't dress up for Halloween," said Zip. "Halloween won't come again until the fall."

"We can go sledding or rafting or trick-or-treating another time," said Kibby. "Let's clean out our closet right now. Then we'll have a head start on next year's New Year's resolution."

明年夏天暖一點的時候才行呢。」

　　茲普從櫃子裡拿出一個手提箱，打開一看，找到了他們的牛仔裝。

　　「我們也不能打扮得像過萬聖節，」茲普說，「要到明年的秋天，萬聖節才會再來。」

　　「我們可以另外找時間玩雪橇，划橡皮艇和玩『不請客，就搗蛋』的萬聖節遊戲，」姬碧說著，「現在先讓我們清理我們的櫃子，這樣的話，我們明年的『新年新希望』就能夠早點開始了呀。」

Because Christmas was coming, Buffy Squirrel wanted to make some presents for her friends.

"I could make a necklace for Kibby," she thought, "if I had some beads. I could also make a hat for Zip if I had some felt."

聖誕節快到了，松鼠芭菲想做一些禮物給她的朋友。

「我可以做條項鍊給姬碧，」芭菲心裡想著，「只要我有些小珠子的話。我也可以做頂帽子給茲普，只要我有些毛料的話。」

芭菲看著她一整年所收藏的東西。有堅果、小樹枝、小圓石、松果等，但就是沒有小珠珠和任何毛料。

Buffy looked at the things she had been collecting all year. She had acorns and twigs, pebbles and pine cones—but no beads and no felt.

"I could make presents out of the things I *do* have," she thought. "If I only had some . . . if I only had some . . . "

What did she need to turn all those things into presents?

"I know!" she cried suddenly. "If I only had some . . . imagination!"

"*And*"—Buffy began to giggle—"some paint and glue."

「哎，我有的這些東西也可以拿來做禮物呀，」她心想，「只要有那麼一點點……只要有那麼一點點……」

她需要什麼一點點就可以把這些東西全都變成禮物呢？

「我知道啦！」她突然大叫，「只要我有那麼一點點的……想像力！」

「再加上，」芭菲開始格格的笑了起來，「一些顏料和膠水啊。」

Buffy wondered if it was silly to collect so many different things.

"Of course, there is a good reason to collect nuts," she thought. "I *eat* nuts. And there is a good reason to collect leaves. I like to sleep on a pile of soft leaves. But there is no good reason to collect other things—like string and paper."

Just then Mother Squirrel came by.

"I cannot wrap any Christmas presents," she said, "until I get some wrapping paper."

"I have some," said Buffy. "I collected all the wrapping paper you used last Christmas. Now you can have it back to use again this Christmas."

芭菲好想知道自己收藏那麼多東西是不是很傻。

「當然啦，我有很好的理由要收集核果，因為我吃核果嘛，」芭菲想著，「我也有很好的理由要收集樹葉，因為我喜歡睡在軟軟的樹葉堆上啊，但是我卻沒有好的理由去收集別的東西，像是細繩和紙張呢。」

正好松鼠媽媽走了過來。

"Thank you, Buffy," said Mother Squirrel. "By the way, you don't happen to have any string for tying up packages, do you?"

「我沒辦法把那些聖誕禮物包起來了，除非我找到一些包裝紙。」她說。

「我有一些呢，」芭菲說，「我把妳去年聖誕節用過的包裝紙，通通都收集起來了。」

「謝謝妳囉，芭菲，」松鼠媽媽說，「對了，妳不會剛好也有用來綁包裹的細線吧?」

Snow fell on Woods Hollow.
It fell on Tall Pine and it fell on Short
Pine. Belvedere Owl was
still predicting fair
weather when the snow
fell on his head.

Grandpa Ground Hog
was asleep in his burrow,
dreaming of spring,
while the snowflakes
were piling up on the
ground above him.

「哈洛小森林」下雪了!

雪落在「大青松」,也落在「小矮松」。貓頭鷹貝弗迪依然預測天氣晴朗,儘管雪已經落到他的頭上了。

土撥鼠老爹在他的洞穴裡呼呼大睡,還夢到了春天呢;外面的雪花早已經在他上頭的地面上堆得高高的。

浣熊洛奇在小木屋內的床上把自己包得緊緊的,正夢見自己被雪困住了呢。

12/
15

Rocky Raccoon was snug in his bed inside Hollow Log, dreaming about being snowed in.

At first the snowflakes came down softly. Then they began to come down faster and faster. They covered the top of Beaver Lodge.

They covered the branches of Oak Tree.

Once again they covered Snow Hill.

　　一開始，雪花是輕輕的飄下來；但沒多久，就愈下愈快。雪把「比弗小木屋」的屋頂都蓋住了；

　　也蓋住了「橡樹」的那些枝椏；

　　就連「雪丘」也再度蓋上一層雪花。

December 16

Zip and Kibby and their friends were playing in the snow.

"Let's have a snowball fight," they said.

Zip took a stick and made a line in the snow. Kibby and Zip made a pile of snowballs on their side of the line. Buffy and Rocky made a pile of snowballs on theirs.

茲普、姬碧和他們的朋友正在雪地裡玩耍。

「我們來打雪仗!」他們說。

茲普拿起一根棍子在雪地上畫出了一條線。姬碧和茲普做了一堆雪球放在線的這一邊;芭菲和洛奇也做了一堆放在線的那一邊。

「這個遊戲要怎麼開始?」芭菲說,「我還不是很想丟雪球呢。」

"How does this game start?" asked Buffy. "I don't feel like throwing snowballs yet."

Just then Zip threw a snowball. It hit Buffy on the arm.

Buffy was surprised. She looked at Zip and laughed.

"*Now* I feel like throwing snowballs!" she cried, and the very first one she threw across the line landed—SMACK!—on Zip.

就在這時候，茲普扔了一個雪球打在芭菲的手臂上。

芭菲嚇了一跳，瞪了茲普一眼，然後笑了起來。

「哈哈，現在我想要丟雪球囉！」她叫著，她扔過界線的第一個雪球就「噗」一聲，狠狠的打在茲普身上。

Down at the bottom of Beaver Pond, the frogs were asleep for the winter. Tad was there, as well as all of the rest of his family.

On a cold December day Mother Frog woke up. She looked around. The water was very dark.

She listened carefully. The water was very quiet.

She stuck her foot out of the mud. The water felt very cold.

Nobody had to tell her that it was not yet time to get up. Not even Father Frog!

She knew perfectly well that she ought to go back to sleep.

And she did.

在「比弗池塘」的池底,青蛙仍在冬眠。泰弟和他的家人也在那裡睡著。

十二月的一個冷天裡,青蛙媽媽醒了過來。她看看四周,池水黑漆漆的;

她仔細的聽聽,水中靜悄悄的;

　　她從泥土裡伸了隻腳出來，唔，水好冷呢！

　　顯然不需要有人來告訴她──包括青蛙爸爸在內──現在還不是起床的時候。

　　她清楚的知道她應該再繼續睡。

　　青蛙媽媽就這樣又睡了。

December 18

Belvedere Owl sat in his weather station, feeling cold and lonely. He felt lonely because of the weather.

He looked up at the sky. The sky was full of big, dark clouds.

"I think we are going to have more snow," said Belvedere. "Even I, the cheeriest weather owl in the forest, have to admit that the weather is going to be bad."

貓頭鷹貝弗迪坐在他的氣象臺裡，心裡覺得又冷又寂寞！就是因為這壞天氣，使他感到孤單。

他抬頭看著天空，天上布滿了濃密的烏雲。

「看來還會下更多的雪了，」貝弗迪說著，「就連我這個森林裡最樂觀的貓頭鷹也不得不承認天氣要轉壞了喲。」

Then Belvedere went down to look in his mailbox. It was full of Christmas cards from all of his friends in Woods Hollow. There was even a Christmas package from some cousins who lived far away.

"This is going to be a fine day after all," said Belvedere Owl.

然後，貝弗迪便下去看看他的信箱。裡面塞滿了聖誕卡，都是所有他在「哈洛小森林」的朋友寄來的；甚至還有聖誕包裹呢，那是一些住在遠方的堂兄弟寄來的。

「嗯，今天的天氣還是不錯的嘛!」貓頭鷹貝弗迪說。

"Tell us a story," said Zip.

"Once upon a time," said Father Chipmunk, "there was a plant who wanted to be a flower. Her name was Poinsettia. Poinsettia had big, beautiful green leaves, but no one paid much attention to her.

"Then one day something wonderful happened. Some of Poinsettia's leaves began to turn red. The red leaves looked just like a flower. Poinsettia's wish to become a flower had come true. But it was even better than she had expected. For not only had she become a flower, but she had become a Christmas flower! Her red and green colors were the colors of Christmas.

「講個故事給我們聽呀。」茲普說。

「以前，」花栗鼠爸爸說，「有一棵植物好想變成一朵花哦，她的名字是『聖誕紅』。她的葉子又大又綠，很漂亮喲！但沒什麼人去注意她。」

「有一天，神奇的事情發生了！『聖誕紅』的葉子有些開始轉紅，紅得看起來就像朵花。她的願望實現了呢！『聖誕紅』變成一朵花啦，而且比她想的還要更好。她不只是變成一朵花，還是一朵聖誕花呢！

12/
19

"And that is why," said Father Chipmunk, "the poinsettia we have at Christmas always reminds me that wishes do come true."

The poinsettia is the Flower of the Month for December.

她身上的鮮紅和翠綠兩種顏色，不就是聖誕節的顏色嗎?」

　　「這就是為什麼，」花栗鼠爸爸說，「在聖誕節的時候，這些聖誕紅都會提醒我一件事：願望終會成真的喲!」

　　　　聖誕紅是代表十二月的花朵

The Chipmunk family were decorating their Christmas tree. Father Chipmunk placed a star on the top. Mother Chipmunk draped Christmas lights on all the branches. Zip and Kibby were stringing popcorn and cranberries.

"Tomorrow is the first day of winter," said Mother Chipmunk. "Do you know what that means?"

"Yes," said Kibby. "The days are getting colder. Soon we will have more snow. The birds will have trouble finding food."

"Do you remember how we gave the birds the popcorn and cranberries last Christmas?" asked Zip. "We can do that again this year."

Zip and Kibby were so eager to give the birds a treat that they made twice as many strings of popcorn and cranberries for the Chipmunk family's tree that Christmas.

花栗鼠全家都在忙著裝飾他們的聖誕樹。花栗鼠爸爸把一顆星星放在樹頂；花栗鼠媽媽在每一根樹枝上掛了聖誕彩燈；茲普和姬碧正把爆米花和小紅莓串起來。

「明天便是今年冬季的第一天，」花栗鼠媽媽說，「你們知道這件事嗎?」

「知道，」姬碧說，「天氣會愈來愈冷，雪也會愈來愈多，鳥兒們

找食物會很困難。」

「妳還記得，我們去年聖誕是怎樣把爆米花和小紅莓拿給那些鳥兒吃的嗎?」茲普問，「我們今年可以再做一次喲。」

茲普和姬碧都想要請鳥兒們好好的吃上一頓，所以這次他們準備了二倍的爆米花加紅莓串，要放在今年花栗鼠家的聖誕樹上呢。

December 21

Zip and Kibby and their friends went caroling a few nights before Christmas. They carried candles to light the way as they went from place to place.

"Today is the first day of winter," Kibby said.

Zip looked up at the stars.

"It looks like the first *night* of winter to me," said Zip.

聖誕前的幾個晚上，茲普、姬碧和他們的那些朋友一家家的去報佳音。他們去每一個地方都帶著蠟燭，以便能把路照得清清楚楚。

「今天是冬季的頭一天喲。」姬碧說了。

茲普往上看著天上的星星說：

「我卻感覺像是冬季的頭一晚呢。」

The carolers sang Christmas songs to Father and Mother Chipmunk. Then they went to Oak Tree and to Beaver Pond.

At last they came to Stone Ledge. Mother and Father Raccoon were happy to hear the singing.

When the carolers had finished, Mother Raccoon gave them cups of hot cocoa to drink.

She did not forget the marshmallows.

這支佳音隊向花栗鼠爸爸、媽媽唱了聖誕歌曲之後，便到「橡樹」和「比弗池塘」去。

最後，他們來到「大岩崖」，浣熊爸爸和媽媽都很高興聽到這些歌聲。

佳音隊獻唱完畢之後，浣熊媽媽給每人喝了一杯熱可可；

當然，她也沒忘了給雪綿糖呢。

December 22

For the past few days Buffy had been busy making presents for her friends. Now she was ready to deliver them.

First she went to see Kibby and Zip.

"Merry Christmas!" said Buffy. "I brought you each a present."

Zip opened his present.
It was a twig hat.
Kibby opened her present.
It was an acorn necklace.
"Thank you, Buffy,"
said Kibby and Zip.

過去的這幾天裡，芭菲一直忙著做禮物送給她的朋友們。現在，她準備好要一一的送出去了。

首先她去看姬碧和茲普。

「聖誕快樂！」芭菲說，「送給你們一人一份禮物。」

茲普打開他的禮物，是一頂樹枝組成的帽子呢。

姬碧打開她的禮物，是一條堅果串成的項鍊哦。

Buffy gave Buck a
pine cone wreath. He
hung it on his door.

She gave Rocky a bag full
of pebble creatures. She had
painted pebbles to look like
beetles. Rocky gave each
beetle a name and made up
stories about them.

Everyone loved Buffy's
presents.

「謝謝妳，芭菲!」姬碧和茲普一起說著。

芭菲送給巴克一個松果編成的花環，巴克立刻把它掛在門上。

她送給洛奇一袋裝滿小圓石做成的動物，她把小圓石塗上各種顏色，看起來像是很多的甲蟲呢。洛奇替每隻甲蟲都取了名字，還為它們編了故事。

每個人都好喜歡芭菲送的禮物喲!

Every now and then something sad happens. There are always a few sad times in every year.

A sad time occurred in Woods Hollow on December twenty-third. Woodsley Bear was going away.

He was wearing his red shirt and his blue hat. He was carrying his large yellow notebook—the notebook that was filled with stories about Woods Hollow.

"Will you ever come back?" asked Zip.

"Of course," said Woodsley, giving Zip a big hug. "I have made many new friends here. I will have to come back to see them again."

"Where are you going now?" asked Kibby.

"I'm going to spend the winter inside my cave," said Woodsley.

悲傷的事情偶爾總會發生一兩件，一年之中也總會有一些令人難過的時候吧。

十二月二十三日，「哈洛小森林」裡發生了一件令人難過的事情，大熊伍史利要離開了！

伍史利穿著他的紅襯衫，戴著他的藍帽子，拿著他那大大的黃色筆記本，筆記本裡已寫滿了「哈洛小森林」的故事。

「你還會回來嗎？」茲普問，

12/
23

"I guess you'll be hibernating the way bears usually do," said Buffy.

"Hibernating?" cried Woodsley as if he had never heard of anything so silly. "I'm not going to sleep all winter. I'm going to write my book about Woods Hollow. There will be a story for every day in the year!"

「當然啦，」伍史利緊緊的抱住茲普說，「我在這裡交了很多新朋友，我一定會再回來看他們的。」

「你現在要去哪裡呢?」姬碧問，

「我要到我的洞穴裡過冬啊。」伍史利說。

芭菲說:「我猜，你也會和別的熊一樣，去冬眠吧。」

「冬眠?」伍史利叫了起來，好像從來沒聽過那麼愚蠢的事一樣，「我才不會把整個冬天拿來睡覺，我要寫下我那本關於『哈洛小森林』的書。這裡面，一年裡的每一天都會有一篇故事喲。」

December 24

It was Christmas Eve at Beaver Lodge. All of the little beavers were tucked into their little beds.

The stockings were hung over the fireplace. The Christmas tree was aglow. Buck was busy putting presents under the tree.

"After I put the presents under the tree," thought Buck, "I will fill the stockings."

聖誕夜囉！在「比弗小木屋」，所有的小河狸都已經蓋好被子在床上睡覺。

壁爐上掛著一排聖誕襪，聖誕樹則亮得通紅。巴克忙著把聖誕禮物擺在樹下。

「等我把禮物擺好後，再去裝那些襪子。」巴克心裡想著。

但過了一會兒，巴克卻睡著了，等他醒來的時候已經很晚了。

But by and by Buck fell asleep. When he woke up, it was very late.

"Oh, my!" said Buck. "It is Christmas Eve and I still have to fill the stockings."

But when Buck looked at the stockings, he was full of wonder. Something magical had happened.

The stockings were already filled.

Someone had come. Who could it have been?

「哎唷，我的天！」巴克說，「已經是聖誕夜了，我還得去裝那些襪子呢。」

但當巴克注視著那些襪子時，他嚇了一跳！不可思議的事情發生了。

襪子都已經裝得滿滿的！

有人來過喲！會是誰呢？

December 25

On Christmas Day in Woods Hollow the Chipmunk family were celebrating at home.

Buck Beaver came to see them, from Beaver Pond.

Rocky Raccoon came to see them, from Stone Ledge.

Buffy Squirrel came to see them, from Oak Tree.

Belvedere Owl flew over from Tall Pine to have a look. The snow had fallen during the night. He saw the tracks of his friends in the snow. They all led right up to the Chipmunk family's front door.

"Hmmm," thought Belvedere. "Everyone is inside where it's warm and cozy and full of Christmas cheer. I think I'll just knock on the door and say Merry Christmas."

聖誕節的那一天，花栗鼠全家都在「哈洛小森林」的家裡歡度佳節。

河狸巴克從「比弗池塘」來拜訪他們；

浣熊洛奇從「大岩崖」來拜訪他們；

松鼠芭菲從「橡樹」來拜訪他們；

貓頭鷹貝弗迪也從「大青松」那邊飛過來看看。雪下了一整個晚

In no time at all Belvedere Owl was inside, too. Everyone was delighted to see him.

There had never been a happier, merrier Christmas in Woods Hollow.

上，所以他可以看到他的朋友們在雪中的腳印，所有的腳印都直通到花栗鼠家的前門。

「嗯，」貝弗迪心想，「每個人都在呢。裡面又暖又舒服，充滿了聖誕節的歡樂氣氛。我想，我就敲敲門說聲聖誕快樂就好了。」

但一下子，貓頭鷹貝弗迪也在屋子裡啦，大家都很高興看見他。

「哈洛小森林」裡從沒有比這更幸福更快樂的聖誕節呢！

精通英語的必備寶典

三民 新英漢辭典

適合在學及進修者

- ↩ 翻譯及重點標示簡單明瞭
- ↩ 總收錄詞目62,400項（詞條43,000項）
- ↩ 附錄「英文文法總整理」，便於查閱了解

豐富詳盡的學習利器

三民 皇冠英漢辭典

針對中學生及
初學者而設計

♻例句豐富、語法詳盡、查閱
方便。
♻插圖幽默生動，輕鬆易懂而
有助記憶。
♻雙色印刷標示醒目，增強學
習效果。

宇宙乾坤 盡在其中

———— 三民中文辭書系列 ————

新辭典

十八開精裝全一冊

滙集古今各科詞語，囊括傳統與現代
詳附各項重要資料，兼具創新與實用

學典

新二十五開精裝全一冊

解說文字淺近易懂，內容富時代性
插圖印刷清晰精美，方便携帶使用